I0628291

AMERICA LOST

**Stories
of
Troublesome Times**

Robert M. Lebovitz

ISBN   978-1-7325045-5-4

AMERICA LOST

Stories
of
Troublesome Times

Other recent fiction by the author:

To Be: *A Novel*
A dystopian view of a future when needs exceed means.

To Be, and Not To Be: The Rise of Misplaced Power and What It May Foreshadow
A three volume ("What Was," "What Is," "What Will Be") dramatization of plundered retirement accounts, Internet-enabled superposition, and geronticide.

We Never Do Wednesday's: Apart Together - A Couple's Alzheimer's Journey
A novel of acceptance.

NUTS! A Fable
A fantasy of the rationalized destruction of tradition, based upon 21st century social/political trends.

*** *!TRUMP!* ***
In Three Acts
A musical parody tracing the path of Donald J. Trump to the Presidency, culminating with his impeachment.

CONTENTS

PREFACE

I'd be pleased if these stories entertain. But, and this is a big but, they were conceived in dark rather than bright moments. They are intended to warm as much as to provide a pleasant afternoon's read. The current milieu is burdened with shadows from the past. These have grown ever darker, more pressing. Much of my literary fiction is shaded in that manner. This is certainly the case for the *To Be, and Not To Be* trilogy, clearly inspired by Orwell's *1984* theme. *We Never Do Wednesday's*, on the other hand, is a partial exception. It's more of a love story. While the narrative traces the inset of Alzheimer's disease, it focuses on how and what it means to survive it.

For a great many, the world isn't a very pleasant place right now. Hopefully, this will moderate as America becomes more aware, reawakens in a sense. That will require thoughtful examination of the world we have built, an analysis based upon verifiable fact not dogma and tempered by accepting that others have as much value as one's self. Perhaps most importantly, it will depend upon leadership that reflects a desire to serve facilitated by but not dominated by a desire for advancement. Even if the policies and programs such a leader would put forth weren't what everyone would prefer, the implied lack of cynical deviousness would allow her/him to offer a net benefit. Putting these stories together is my way of attempting to illustrate that the first step in moving any society forward is to be aware of its flaws and to feel their urgency.

The economy and national prospects were bright as this decade opened. Yet, there were ample reasons for an undercurrent of ill-ease: the slow but inexorable growth in income and wealth disparity; the burgeoning cost of health care coupled with its increasingly mercantile nature; a growing concern for the viability of entitlement (safety net) programs; a documented environmental crisis instantiated by storms, droughts, and fires; the risks implied (and recently demonstrated) by our increasing dependence upon foreign goods correlated with compromised productive resilience. To season these concerns, we've had the spice of three major financial crises over a span of only twenty years. The global pandemic of 2020 is particularly noteworthy. Of course, business prospects are cyclic. Economies endure then recover from periodic corrections. For wage earners and the owners of small businesses, however, the impact of COVID-19 rivals that of the 1929 crash and its aftermath. There are fears, now, of a similar, prolonged economic slowdown.

The mature and the well-positioned will ride this disturbance out. They may recover most if not all of what they lost and even go beyond. But for a great many — especially those just starting out — this is a life changing event. A profoundly negative impact on expectations and, therefore, attitude will follow. While federal monetary and fiscal policies have been initiated to hasten a return to "normalcy"

PREFACE

(as Warren Harding chose to put it), the severity of the complex of problems suggests that substantial recovery will take years rather than months. Many now face the fears and uncertainties that once afflicted a few. The accompanying loss of confidence, especially among the young, is worrisome. Broadly shared economic advancement and democracy reinforce each other. They may, in fact, be critically interdependent. The longer it takes to emerge from this morass, the more likely it becomes for that disaffection to expand and yield a loss of popular support. Such is fertile ground for autocracy.

The short tales in this collection were written well before 2020, but with grave misgivings as to the nature of societal trends already in mind. The pandemic of 2020 and the financial crisis (dare I suggest crises?) that has(have) resulted, or yet may, are analogous to the disturbed world of my dystopian trilogy, *To Be and Not To Be*. The events dramatized in that novel are plausible and mirror present-day, factual concerns: reduced confidence in the dollar and U.S. sovereign debt (a rational reaction to the twin specters of an actual depression and the fear of a looming insolvency); restricted access to private retirement funds (or sequestration or expropriation or taxation of assets, each of which amounts to the same); a validation of far-right ideology (the result of implicit political support); massive governmental oversight and compromised privacy (as in personal tracking couched in terms of overriding broad societal benefit); plus geronticide (a new calculus for life and death in ICUs and senior facilities based upon necessitated allocation of limited resources). The precise details of their instigation are secondary. In profound crises, similar needs often arise from diverse precursors.

The earliest story, "Stone," dates from 2009. The latest, "Wilderness," came about after reading of yet another mass shooting. Several were conceived while working on the first version of *To Be*, a 2013 private printing. Others were elaborated upon and, with modifications, incorporated in the 2018 trade edition of *To Be, and Not To Be*. Overall, the tales shared here represent quite a departure from the anthropomorphic *NUTS!* fable and the three act musical play/parody *** *!TRUMP!* ***. All, however, are suited to the period following the election of 2016, which could be characterized by an enhanced, often politically driven tolerance for conflict and antagonism mediated via the Internet and, in part, the result of a perception of the decline in personal income and enhancement of dependencies that globalization has come to impose upon many.

The appearance of a virulent bacterium or virus that produces a pandemic has been visited often in literature. The fictional endings are usually happy, with the plot resolved through heroic vanquishment of the scourge. As history reveals, however, reality is not so simple. As of this writing COVID-19 has created enormous dislocations. Where these will lead us is difficult to ascertain. History teaches, however, that we should not be overly sanguine. Social disruption is often a precursor to fundamental political change. We may be on the cusp of a major transition. The national character with which we are familiar — democracy flourishing amidst capitalism — may be poised for fundamental not cosmetic modification.

Academic surveys of the political scene are still exploring the long-standing conflict between capitalism, with its maximization of utility and profit, and socialism, with its focus on leveling. This is a valid historical battleground, no doubt, but one littered with the remains of an earlier era, the corpses, if you will, of eighteenth and nineteenth century ideas. In this century, there will be no winner in those terms. Technological developments, particularly AI and the Internet, assure us of that. Rather, something quite new will arise, something the details of which are fuzzy, as is usually the case in times of dramatic societal stress. Modern capitalism's broadly elevating acquisitiveness has given rise to a new imperative, that of consumption for its own sake. The mismatch between what is implicitly promised and what can be explicitly attained has been exposed and will become progressively more pressing. Whether from feeling demonstrably deprived or simply from the fear of losing privilege gained, many will experience enhanced levels of stress. A bloom of wide spread, already rooted anomie is the inevitable result.

The future is unknown but is certain to engender anxiety. Neither short term palliation nor magical thinking will serve. To fully recover, we will need thoughtful public participation, wise leadership grounded on verifiable facts not fantasies, and the good fortune to be spared further "black swans." There appears to be a sense of ill-ease, an apperception of uncertainty, a general concern for the security that all seek for themselves and for those close to them, which are likely to be part of our social fabric for some time to come. These are troublesome times, indeed, a time of transition.

There always will be discontents. However, action requires some concept or event to mobilize and energize latent intention(s). The viral pandemic of 2020 has provided such a catalyst. Success will come to those who recognize the strategic potential of the associated stress, devise the tactics to mobilize it, and pursue, with single-minded persistence, their suddenly more realizable goals, which may or may not be the same as those of their recruits. This summarizes the turning point that the year 2020 may represent. What we are seeing now, in relatively small doses, could be but a preview of what will loom large should the crisis persist or, worse, be exacerbated by those who see it as an opportunity to make more popular their heretofore fringe cause(s). Whether the nation will emerge strengthened or diminished remains to be seen.

The titular tale dates from several years ago and was, in fact, incorporated in a chapter ("Venice in the Sun") of *To Be, and Not To Be.* Yet, it resonates with recent events. If, when exercising their democratic right to protest, peacefully assembled protestors (Washington, D.C.) and an elderly white man (Buffalo, N.Y.) can be brutalized by those sworn to uphold the law, then what chance did/does a person of different color, of different beliefs, or of different sexual orientation have (too numerous to cite)? What is done to the least of us is done to all of us. Having "America Lost" open the collection is thus fitting, in view of a suddenly compromised national future with much to overcome, not the least of which is a debasement of the democratic spirit of compromise and civility.

After all, historical and current events alike demonstrate that overt class conflict, fraudulent voting, and financial deprivation are not necessities for weaponizing discontent. Insecurity — social, political, and/or economic — is sufficient.

Spring 2020

AMERICA LOST

The facile rationalization of antipathy.

AMERICA LOST

After a string of sullen gray days has come one bright and sunny, a day such as the Chamber of Commerce promises is the norm for Southern California. From his window Marcel sees no low fog, no drizzle, no evidence of discouraging onshore wind. Calm and warm, it's perfect for his exploratory stroll. Afterward he'll read or watch soccer from Europe, then throw together a casual Saturday dinner. Something Mediterranean would be nice, he imagines as he walks to the residence's singular elevator. He has leftover lamb and slices of eggplant he could sauté. Also, there's a box of couscous that he should use up before it gets buggy. No one's fault, the presence of those mobile specs, he surmises. Grain weevil eggs were already in the box when he bought it months ago. Invisible, but there. Sated and waiting.

Marcel lets out a soft sigh. Without having finalized any plan, he has arrived at the stop just as his bus is pulling up. Sitting on the right, facing away from the afternoon sun, he stares out, with neither aim nor focus. He prefers the internal quiet that his regular, solitary outings should encourage but seldom provides. His transfer to the #1 at Main is well timed. When the bus jerks to a stop along the circle in Venice, he cues the young woman to go ahead. With a second casual wave, in response to her deferential nod, he wordlessly insists. Unmasked relief reveals that she has anticipated he would walk slowly and cause tedious delay, as do most elderly. It transforms his urbane courtesy into a confirmation of her presumption, which, justifiable or not, is unwelcome. Hers was a look that he's neither used to nor desires to foster.

He follows her down the aisle, shoulders back and watching her bag, carried on a long shoulder strap, pummel the chrome seat frames. He eyes her mobile, tightly swathed hips as compensation for the prior implied slight. He strides purposefully, avoiding use of the hand rail or seat backs for confidence-building support. He grips the post as he exits, however, to swing down over the last step, landing with bent knees as once he was instructed. Erect, military in his mind, and to further discount his age, he increases his pace to pass the young woman, who is by then intent upon her cell phone. Both follow the curve along to Windward, he intent primarily upon increasing the distance between them.

Once beyond the leafy canopy he squints, sunglasses momentarily inadequate. Thus reminded, he retrieves the stiff-beaked, white cap from his jacket pocket. Pulling it down at the back, to avoid inadvertent hat hair, he notes the overgrown empty lot on his left. It elicits memories of his late wife and their customary corner table, of their enjoying a virtuous meatless dinner after an exhilarating day of sailing, of familiar servers and the very old-word manner of the owner. That would have been during those fast paced, mutually focused few years BC — before children. Other recollections emerge, which he pushes aside, except for the linked thought of why, after so many years of success, their special place had closed. He still has no answer. Everything since in the same space, in serial tests of new ideas and high hopes, had failed. Even the building is gone, as is she, he notes reflexively. The thought stings but less so in recent years.

Ahead, in the shadows provided by distressed Californian nee Mexican imitation of Spanish colonnade on either side of Pacific, the tourist shops are busy. Getting less sun today, he decides would be a wise idea. Without looking he rubs the dry skin on the back of one hand with the other. She had always encouraged him to use lotion daily, as did she. When he gets home, after his shower, he will, he silently promises.

Hurrying with demonstrative haste across Windward at mid-block, he heads in the covered walkway's direction.. The officer at the corner gives him a disapproving scowl but seems to have more pressing matters to attend to, made evident by his uninterrupted conversation into the microphone attached to his helmet. The police cars he had barely noticed parked around the circle behind suddenly becomes part of a pattern, forms an evocative scene. Marcel sees two others stationed not far ahead, along Windward itself. Several more are to his right, north, along Pacific Avenue. He waves an apology to the nearest officer, meant to confirm that he won't repeat the infraction. He needn't have bothered. The man is preoccupied and disinclined to chastise. Something has happened or is about to, it is fair to judge, Marcel concludes.

It was a few years ago, about when Doctor Laufer retired, and he remembers it well. It could have been he who was maimed or killed by the car that sped along the paved walkway that borders the level sand at the back of Venice Beach. He had frequented the area enough, especially when getting used to being alone. Generally known as the Boardwalk, despite that the hard-surface provides the very antithesis of yielding wood in sound as well as feel underfoot, it's populated with an irregular array of stalls, carts, and display tables — often hastily assembled — on either side for many blocks and thus is popular with strolling locals and tourists. After that vehicular rampage, sturdier barriers were installed to reinforce its designation as a pedestrian walkway. Vehicular access nevertheless had to remain relatively easy, however, to accommodate service trucks and police cars.

He surveys the officers' presence and toys with the idea that a similar incursion could have occurred earlier today. Or, considering that the current political and financial stresses are so acute, it would be no surprise if some violent street protest had taken place or is about to. Perhaps a terrorist threat has been received. Nothing appears amiss, however.

The officers are watchful but sedate. No ambulances, news groupies, or clusters of curious onlookers are evident. The street and sidewalks are innocent of debris. Yet, they wouldn't be so alert without a reason, Marcel starts to consider as he looks about. Approaching the corner, the walk signal is in his favor, which takes precedence. He neither expects nor needs a clear resolution to the vague contradictions and quickly focuses on making his escape across the busy street, which is constricted by sawhorse barricades set up in the far curbside lane.

Beachy's is open and busy. The glass doors of the stereotypical coastal emporium are opened outward, held there by baker's racks of the cheap trivia made for pennies abroad and destined to be sold here for dollars. There are plastic figures on sticks, hanging samples of inflatables that should, if treated with respect, survive at least an afternoon without leaking or splitting. Without explicit investigation on this day, he knows that inside are plates, mugs, and hats individualistically embroidered with "Life's a Beach!" or "Venice, California" or "Santa Monica Yacht Harbor" or even simply "Hollywood!" in a selection of fonts and colors. Out of sight to him are similarly annotated tops, plus garish sundresses and cheap bathing suits next to low quality polyester towels and colorful, branded beach pails. No question but that pins, pens, pullovers, and posters are prominently displayed within. As on previous forays, he smiles at the unfathomable attraction of the inscrutable anime figures secured to key rings, by which they hang on the rotating rack by the entry. Marcel's final glance through the shop's side windows lingers on long, thick pencils variously topped with plastic orcas in mid-leap, cruising dolphins, upright seals, or jiggly, hirsute pastel orbs.

The offerings on Ocean Front Walk itself, just beyond the intersection at Speedway not far ahead, will include many nearly equivalent mementos, as he also is aware from prior visits. The tawdry trifles evidently provide sufficient reward for all, from inception and manufacture through jobber then retailer, to encourage their diligence. Colorful, cheap, destined to be soon discarded and forgotten. Perhaps that's why people buy them, he thinks — to gratify a carefully orchestrated impulse. Made pensive by that notion but glad to be freed of prior thoughts, he focuses more on the people as he continues along Windward.

Across the street a tight group, all in bathing suits with towels over their shoulders, is arranging for rental of beach gear: short-legged beach chairs; rickety umbrellas; boogie boards, and, if adventurous, heavily scuffed long-boards. Nearby, an array of neglected bicycles and scooters await specific interest. An eruption of children from the yogurt shop, their drippy cones dangerously askew, brings Marcel to a cautious standstill. He responds with his own to the broadcast smiles of the harried couple in charge. While his memories are distant, dim, and ambiguous, he can relate. He even thinks of tomorrow being Sunday, the day they usually call. It's enough to prolong his small smile. Approaching the twin lines of skinny, rough trunks at Speedway, he looks up at the palms' sagging, minimally disturbed fronds. The breeze is light and, blending with the fall Southern California sun, feels good on his skin. He lets his smile fade.

Most here are young and most are proceeding, as is he, nominally westward toward the beach frontage, i.e., to Ocean Front Walk, the Boardwalk, which appellation has stuck irregardless of its vague applicability. On his way across, his curiosity resurrected, he studies the lineup of Santa Monica Police Minis, the nearest topped with a neat row of helmets. Uniformed officers are scattered about, seemingly less focused on their surroundings than on their logo embellished coffee cups and each other. He looks along the street in the opposite direction and spots a lone, stationary cruiser, a blue-sleeved arm casually dangling from the driver's window.

Accepting that unusual does not imply dire, he walks on, toward the sand and the ever active surf beyond. Hot dogs at a nearby stand, rotating under a heat lamp in the old-fashioned but eminently practical manner, are too pale, too wrinkled. Nevertheless, their scent has the intended effect. He must swallow as he approaches but continues past without stopping. Having passed the test, having overcome this, his first temptation, Marcel makes a mental note to focus less on the food, or the officers, and more on the early afternoon strollers.

At the edge of the sand, standing motionless to absorb the various impressions, he peers along the many vendor stalls that define Ocean Front Walk. Essentially unchanged for years, for decades, only the occupants and their wares are periodically renewed. Of corrugated metal, propped up canvas, and plywood, with their security fronts raised barely above eye level for a tall person, which he is not, they're permanently temporary. Most of the dim interiors display jumbled assemblages of low-priced wares, which, while necessarily imported as claimed and better than the earlier crass tourist junk, are of dubious authenticity as well as quality. Also, there are tattoo artists, sweets sellers, and boutiques each displaying a plethora of cheap sweaters and tees. Passably useful junque is for sale, along with games, toys, and decorative imports, the best of the last often with interesting ethnic individuality.

All in all, Marcel enjoys the Venice Boardwalk much more than the stupefyingly repetitive corporate shops of central Santa Monica. In addition to its vendors with diverse origins, there are sun-worshiping tourists and already tanned locals worth observing. The skate park, for example, just ahead, is in active use, as usual. He heads in its direction, across the sand to the concrete Strand, where he easily locates an empty bench from which to watch both the acrobatics on small wheels and the diverse panorama provided by the busy throng. The sound of atypically heavy surf comes from beyond the berm. He examines the horizon with a sailor's eye. More wind, westerly, he determines, with perhaps some rain tomorrow. The clouds are very dark and piled high but at the edge of the earth. No storm today, but soon enough. Marcel can't see the swash, hidden as it is by that final rise before the water's edge. He can, however, see the loose assemblage of surfers beyond.

Dark torsos, with legs straddling nose-up surfboards, alertly wait. Others, also protected by wetsuits, push through collapsing curls, ride over boiling white, or lay themselves flat to stroke toward building fronts of gray-green where they turn about, hop up, and strain for the reward of a brisk ride. In today's active surf, many flail and fall, disappearing briefly under the froth. Forcing his eyelids into slits doesn't help him see the details of the riders and the waiters. All are beyond easy scrutiny. He shifts his gaze to the sea-hugging bank of dark clouds on the horizon. Soon, yes, he thinks. It would be wise to avoid that, too.

The surfers too small in the distance to be compelling, it takes only a few minutes for Marcel to tire of the hectic looping and jumping of the nearby hunched figures on their wheeled boards. He shifts his interest to the softly curved, narrow, concrete Strand itself. Sampling each direction, he endeavors to isolate a worthwhile sojourner, someone either tantalizingly shapely or curiously strange, to follow with his eyes. With today's fine weather, the level of activity is as expected. Youthful vigor passes by in a steady, random parade: runners and walkers, couples and singles, blade gliders and bikers. Thus prompted, he looks down, at the back of his hands, at his old skin. After pushing aside a fold with his thumb, he watches it drift back into place. There was a time, Marcel pointlessly recalls, when it would snap back promptly. He makes a fist and runs the side of his thumb along the triplet of parallel blue worms, watching them collapse then refill and thinking of the times a nurse had searched for a productive vein. In an instant of decision, his extends his fingers and slaps the tops of his knees to propel himself to his feet. He strides along the serpentine path, partially retracing his steps, then continues south, toward Muscle Beach, the rec center, and the volleyball pits, hoping for a girls' match.

"On your left!" he hears and instinctively veers to starboard. The whir of the biker's passing is too close.

"Bastarda imprudente!" he throws at her but softly, so as not to fully engage. Judging that there will be other inconsiderate fools, he continues to hug the right edge of the meandering solid path.

The afternoon sun is weaker than a few months ago but still dazzling by the beach. He pulls down the bill of his ball cap. It helps, enables him to avoid squinting. There are no benches at the ersatz oasis of tall palms set upon the grassy knoll ahead. Their skinny, bare trunks offer no shade, which perhaps explains that observable. A homeless person — this isn't the first time Marcel has encountered him — lies on the lee slope of the knoll amidst dirty quilts. Its hooded sweatshirt leaves nothing exposed, which is incongruous among the so scantily clad. Marcel's focus shift to the sharp shouts farther along and the ringing thumps of an inflated ball slamming against concrete capture. He walks on more rapidly, stopping near six twenty-somethings standing idle, one holding a basketball in the crook of his arm. Having recently concluded their contest, their tees moist and clinging, they are watching a fresh sextet dart about. With, but not because of his approach, three of the former break away and walk out onto the sand.

Having no agenda, Marcel mimics those remaining. He watches the players weave about, dribble, leap, and shoot. In cutoffs and sleeveless pullovers, their muscles are like supple apples beneath their melanic skin. There are loud shouts and high fives; their competition is serious. Even from a distance, he ruefully admires their sweaty athleticism. However, being a passive observer with little real empathy for the sport, he soon resumes his walk. The departing trio, strolling not far ahead, has returned to the hard surface of the walk/bikeway after one failed to force their worn orange ball to bounce up from the pliant sand. He smirks and flips it to a companion then peels off his shirt, uses it to wipe his ebony head.

Trailing at a distance, Marcel takes in the contrasting sedateness of the tennis courts, which are mostly hidden by the scrim-covered fence. He hears rhythmic thwacks and thwops interspersed with rubbery squeaks. An occasional grunt or a sharp cry of "Out!" is the only human sound.

That was a sport that he had often regretted not having tried. It would have provided great exercise, had he been enthused by a like-minded partner.

Without pausing, he takes in the musclemen's platform. Today the graduated rows of benches facing it, in front of the weight pit, are empty. The next big event won't be held until the holidays, or possibly sooner, on Halloween. A lone, muscular black man dangles from a pull-up bar, eyes closed and waiting, his chest expanding and collapsing rhythmically, which Marcel finds analogous to the ocean's quasi-periodic slow swells.

Further along are the beach volleyball courts. Agreeably, there is a mixed doubles match in progress. He stops to admire the uncomplicated attractiveness of the well-proportioned youths facing off in pairs on either side of the high net — their large sunglasses, the narrow waists and broad shoulders of the boys, the skimpy suits of the girls and their long, tight, blond braids. As they dive and dig, he twists his torso in sympathy. The near girl has a fine shape. Her next service hits the net. Her partner pulls at the waist of his loose trunks and hangs his head as he kicks the ball ahead. They must be losing, Marcel decides. The unsuccessful server leans forward, forearms on tense, ample thighs, running a finger under the lower edge of her bikini bottom while waiting. Yes, he thinks, a very fine shape. He pulls his ball cap down, partly to make it secure against any gust but more to hide his eyes. After several exchanges of service he feels too much like an interloper, a voyeur, in fact. Facing away from the sound of yet another open-handed slap as he walks on, he hears the clatter of a drumbeat from the parking lot ahead and the confusion of many youthful voices. He sees again the three black ex-basketball players, who have anticipated his ramble and are already onto the pocked paved area occupied by the gathering.

Suspended from two poles jammed into the adjacent sand, a banner sags in loose folds between its supports, which, coupled with a complicated font, makes it difficult to read. A snatch of breeze puffs out the cloth so he can. "One Country Under God," he extracts from the complicated Gothic script. Marcel ponders the three or four dozen young people milling about, many in the process of emptying plastic bottles to replenish themselves. The males — in collared white shirts and black pants — are gathering signage into manageable sets as they chatter. Their no longer crisp black and white attire, virtual uniforms, provide him a further and sufficient clue:

The parking lot is the designated terminus of a march, it seems. Their counterparts, the females, who seem to have little to do, are in scattered threes and fours. Most have their hair short or, if long, pulled tight into prim pony tails. Some wear scarves tied under their chins. Nearby, double-faced sign boards stand upright, each removed from the shoulders of some now tired enthusiast. Pole cards also are in evidence, either inverted and leaning upon the side of a dull colored, dusty van or lying flat on the ground next to it. All, except for that cloth banner, are of poster board and share a crisp, unadorned font in flat black upon stark white.

He scans a few, filling in where there is overlap: "Choose Christ" and "The Bible is Tru–"

"'... is True' or '... is Truth,'" Marcel ventures under his breath.

Another starkly commands: "!*BELIEVE*!"

Some of the placards are formatted as two lines of text — for poetic effect, it would appear. One has the second word of each line in bold, for added emphasis: "Make **Christ** Your Partner / In **Life** and Beyond."

The men are young, with either closely cropped hair — service, not recruit style — or with their pates shaved clean. The latter isn't this afternoon's affectation. Otherwise, hours in the sun would have left their heads a rosy pink. Only sweat adorns them. A few have electronic bullhorns beside them, resting on their wide mouths. Those in a tight huddle about a notably neater and more mature comrade, apparently an organizer, are captivated by the pen he lets drift down along a clipboard. The bold swastika on its backside is made of tape, the kind shiny and black that electricians use. Once signifying love and life, it's become the glyph of hate and death. Nearby, a half dozen or so grip a limp flag, which is so collapsed that only its familiar, bold colors are identifiable. Their free hands pressed to their chests, they stand with eyes lowered, lips moving.

On top of a second pile is the aphorism that, sadly, seems particularly apt at the moment: "To Obey Is To Love."

Marcel emits a sigh of understanding, projecting that the opposite face of this card would no doubt display the inverse of that admonition. Theirs is a march that comes at a time of unrest and fear, a time of social discontent engendered by financial stress and fueled by political manipulation. What has long been suppressed has been released, provided with justification hence the right to be honored. Its aim is to encourage trading away the uncertainties of freedom for the infallibility of authority, irrespective of any prior civil liberalism.

"'The only thing we have to need is ... need itself,'" he whispers, as if it is a direct quote and not merely a parody of the marchers' method, or rather, of that of their minders. The original was something he had read of decades ago, a lifetime ago, when studying for citizenship, soon after arriving from

Buenos Aires and before doing a second residency in the Navy.

"Hah," he scoffs. "Fear's their gateway, their means."

At last he grasps the reason for the many police cars. This serious march probably started at the park on Westchester, instead of ending there like last year. Rather than using Pacific Avenue, it came down Speedway and, as suggested by the placement of the barriers, partway down the Boardwalk. On that prior occasion the police were fully occupied, first with the parade's tying up traffic, then with the unorganized rowdies' subsequent opportunism. Today's restricted route simplified their oversight but must have caused confusion among the tourists as well as the vendors. Marcel feels fortunate to have missed it.

One of the assembly slings a bullhorn over his shoulder by its lanyard then unfurls a strip of tricolored bunting from its pair of standards. He signals a companion to take up the other. "March With Us To Affirm Your America" is emblazoned on the fringed cloth. For a last, proud instant, it is stretched out full length, more than the width of a lane of traffic. From its size and the bright gold of its edging, Marcel surmises that this had been carried foremost, the theme of their parade. With a third person gripping its midpoint to assist, the banner is rolled up but not before Marcel absorbs the revivified symbols that bracket the phrase. Bullhorn bouncing at his side, the fellow slings the pair of poles with their secured banner under his arm and strides to the rear of the unwashed van.

They have finished their parade of show and exhortation, and are dispersing. While Marcel is unfamiliar with the details of their lives, he is convinced that few of those here will ever clamber beyond the status of hourly service. Instilled with a firm rejection of those who might, most will never overcome the limitations of virtual satisfactions and guided consumption. Here they have gathered, professing their faith in the wonder of knowing without doubt, of identifying without examining. He shakes his head, in slow, sad acknowledgment of how primitive yet powerful must be the satisfaction that derives from acting out what they has been programmed to believe.

The unparsed murmuring from those nearby is interrupted by loud voices beyond. Those whom he earlier had been trailing stand in a rough line, with the grounded basketball a symbolic barrier in front of them. Former marchers, in their white shirts and black slacks, surround one of their own, who is strapped to a large drum. They are crowding him back. Infused with Muscular Christianity, he isn't about to let some predefined miscreants' intrusion go unanswered. There are words, angry words, which Marcel is too distant to make out. They are related, no doubt, to those recidivist nationalist symbols that he glimpsed on the banner and now sees again on the drumhead.

Necks are stiff; heads are thrust forward. The three in transit are clearly outnumbered but hardened by experience. Those in opposition possess the strength provided by uniformity made palatable by repeated drill and exigency. One of the sweat-stained trio picks up the ball and starts to leave. His black companions follow. There are short, sharp, derogatory exclamations, which cause the former to wheel around. He yells something, which he then repeats more loudly while appending an exclamatory hand gesture. A large wave simultaneously comes to its noisy end, else Marcel might have been able to make out that reply. The basketball player's friends, standing with fists on canted hips, look on passively. The closest puts an open hand to his mouth to shout, no doubt to coax his companion away from the uneven confrontation. With comparable though less necessary intent, the arm of the erstwhile drummer is tugged by a compatriot. The moment passes. Each side reconnects with their respective lives, their intended tasks, their directed misdirections.

With nothing further to observe, feeling profoundly overexposed to the marchers and their agenda, Marcel returns to the paved beach path. He takes possession of a bench that's close to the volleyball court but faces out toward the water. Facing away from the lithe athletes, he disregards their occasional shouts and instead scrutinizes the activity along the Strand. Unfortunately, he finds it difficult to leave the marchers behind, not easy to instead focus on the parade of variety on the walkway in front of him: the striders and strollers; the runners and rollers. With arms extended along the top rail of the fortuitous bench, he lifts his chin to the sky, feels the cushion of compressed flesh at the back of his neck, and hears a gentle crunch. He rolls his head and attempts to achieve inner silence.

The sun warm on his face, the breeze pleasant, and his thoughts having relented, Marcel opens his eyes to the increasingly active flow along the Strand. He is rewarded by an almost steady stream, much of it youthfully attractive. The few who approximate his seniority often nod or offer a small smile. Others, blank-faced if alone and often when they aren't, share an affection for firmly implanted earbuds. With the sun warm upon him, pleasant feelings are revived. He serially, discreetly, watches nubile girls cruise by, admiring their taut, youthful bodies and judging the novelty of their chosen modes. No one pays him any mind. Safe, eyes hidden by his sunglasses, he takes in their breasts and the fluid bulk of their thighs, the latter often deliciously indented by a tight bathing suit or shorts, as they approach. Then, prudently, he evaluates their glutei as they move away. He scouts for the paired hollows often found just above the waist, which high sun would make his wife's so prominent. His past again intruding, he relents to it, allows the image of her standing near the mast of their long-gone sail boat, steadied by it and laughing with him at the unexpected gasp of a dolphin close to port. Aided by the surf's tentatively regular beat, he tries to make the memory more real, to make it come alive. He can't and wishes he hadn't let it come to him at all.

Many minutes pass. Shoulders stiff from the enforced casualness of his spread eagle position, Marcel brings his hands down to his lap. He studies first their palms then their reverse, noting how his skin is pleasantly tanned from years in the sun. It is also, however, blemished and dry. The slant light accentuates the fine patchwork of wrinkles that solidifies the separation between him and those whom he has been watching. It's as wide as the gulf between him and his variegated past, and as unbridgeable.

"Time. Can't be stopped or turned back," he whispers, immediately feeling self-conscious and grateful for the noise of the surf as he looks to either side.

The breeze and the surf slacken. In the gap he hears the faint babble of voices, angry voices it seems, and faint crackling noises amid shouts. With little incentive to investigate, he rolls his eyes skyward then slowly down again, to scan the sea to what is colloquially referenced as being "the west." The clouds have drifted closer. They are taller and darker, he discerns.

Finally, Marcel senses that he has been sitting long enough. It's time, he feels, to catch the bus for home. Upright, he feels the wind, that it has become brisker. Glad for his light jacket, he takes the cutback to the Boardwalk. A gangling young man with a spiky mohawk and wearing tattered jeans stands near an oil barrel trash bin. It is gaudily painted and anointed with black graffiti. Taken together they are the epitome of irrelevance, relics soon to be extinct, soon to be intolerable vestiges of independence, even here, at Venice Beach.

Just past the concrete cubicles of the restrooms, he emerges onto the tenuous exhibitionism of the Boardwalk. A vendor's stock of sunglasses, in a myriad of shades and shapes and each in its own white plastic compartment on a slanted rack, would be worthy of a photo were it not that similar matrices are so often found on beachfront commercial strips. "CLIP ON!" screams the intentionally overwrought signage. "ONE PRICE!" with none given, states another.

He grins at the "Welcome, Friends And Fiends" over a green-painted entrance flanked by locked cases of glass bongs. Each of the recreational/medical appliances in the diminutive museum is artistically complex, deceptively benign, and dusty with the fine particles that have encroached upon the display through cracks and seams. "High People Are Happy People!" proclaims the calligraphic script on a 3x5 card positioned among them.

It being a pleasant weekend afternoon, the pedestrian walkway is busy. Some of the vendor stalls, however, are closed, which is surprising at this hour, with this many people about. Before Marcel can digest this and relate it to anything he had earlier observed or has just heard, he notices a gathering of middle-aged men under an oversize Henna Tattoos sign. They are agitated, it would seem, talking earnestly and staring toward the tall thin palms, past which he had recently come and is now returning. Marcel slows to eavesdrop.

"Not many. Five or six of 'em. Sure made a big mess," a scruffy gentleman says, gesturing with both hands. The wizened speaker pulls out a red checked cloth, gray at the margins. He blows his nose into it then stuffs it forcefully into his pocket.

Marcel resumes his slow trek toward the imputed commotion. On the way he passes still open stalls with their proprietors ready to serve. An collection of pop art — Goth, Cartoon, Sci Fi, Fantasy — has attracted a foursome of swarthy men in long robes who are gurgling undecipherable comments to each other. Further on, casual shoes and sandals sit in a semi-organized pile atop a table. It's too late in the season for the beach and walkways to become uncomfortably hot, which accounts in part for the scant interest they have drawn. On the other hand, the adjacent "You're name on a grain of rice" man has a pair of young customers waiting. His implied artisanal prowess is apparently unsullied by the erroneous grammar.

Still a few dozen steps from the tall palms at Windward, Marcel sees an exceedingly thin fellow, squatting on his haunches, whom he hadn't noticed when he earlier passed this way. The keening man is the focus of a clutch of silent onlookers. With arms flexed back along either side of his head and hands dangling, his too white eyes scan the limpid orange and black remnants that surround him.

"... do nothing," he is saying.

There are black cats of cardboard, cell paper, and crepe with legs torn off or at crazy angles. There are the broken bones of paper skeletons. Plastic pumpkins with fanciful features — the formerly smooth, globular decorations now jagged and flattened — lie about at odd angles, grinning. Multicolored streamers are heaped in disorder, like a seamstress's discards.

"They do nothing," the crouched vendor says again, as if he has grown tired from repeating it.

Marcel stops and tries to extract the essence of the scene. A glimpse of two broken signs, each bent in half next to the intensely black man, provides context: "Halloween - Here," Marcel reads. "Big Sale!!!" Conical hats, broken bags of candies, edible figurines in cellophane, also broken and stomped, a scattering of familiar, therefore not frightful masks — all that might be offered during a few weeks in late October — lie destroyed and scattered, smashed and torn near the overturned table of the skin and bones black man with the very white eyes and dark lips tight over very white teeth. A half inflated bright vinyl pumpkin — its mouth a misshapen black gash — stares up with painted eyes, a mocking, orange confederate also trying to grasp what has taken place and why.

"The policeman, they stand, do nothing. They do nothing. What I do wrong?"

Marcel realizes the man is looking up at him, addressing him specifically and demanding an answer, some explanation. Having neither, unable to respond to the importuning, he retreats a step, chagrined to realize that he'd been so sadly staring down as if to offer a personal apology, that he'd been so obvious in his attempt to understand.

"What I do wrong? Toys an' candies. Just toys an' candies," the black man sobs.

His thin arms tighten about his head. The storm of righteousness has passed. It has wiped away his meager means to provide. Marcel cannot begin to offer anything to the man whose family undoubtedly will share his pain. Yet, he will retain his visceral sense of the scene and deconstruct it later, probably tonight. The unfortunate will be his muse for an hour or so of imagined insight, little more. Words would not change any of it, now or then. The poor African and his plight are symptoms, signposts of reordering. Turning away, Marcel rejoins the casual busyness of the Boardwalk.

The scent of sausages wafts over him as he recrosses Windward. A clever vendor has positioned a fan next to the red-hued glass case holding impaled, glistening morsels of "ALL BEEF! Spicy, Mild, Jalapeno, or Cheese" rounds. Tempted, Marcel once again must suppress unwise desire. He does come to a stop, however, because of his recollection of the "Eat of This" vendor who used to have this well-located spot. He reimages the Mideastern food that had been the pleasant young man's specialty: kofta — always lamb, never beef — plump triangles of kuku sabzi, jujeh and kibbeh, falafel. He would arrange spoonfuls of smooth tahini, spicy dukkah, baba ghanouj rich with oil, or moist tabuleh upon flatbread, adding pungent chunks of the meat for those who might want a stand-up meal more than an exotic snack. His had been a popular stand until xenophobic protestors made their periodic appearance. Marcel had always chosen the cheese over the spinach fatayer, but never by name. That was unnecessary. The choices had reminded him of the street food when he was a boy in a vastly different culture. He would point to his preferred amber-topped tricorn, content with the unlikelihood of retaining a then newly experienced culture's unique appellations.

Marcel lifts his head, sniffing for a hint of harissa, of cumin, or of hot garlic. All are gone, replaced by the aroma of common cured meat. "Another marker. Another signpost," he thinks very deliberately and with a palpable measure of sadness.

Resigned to the current imperative to forgo, he continues on, passing by stalls featuring overly familiar collections of beachy souvenirs. There are seashells, shoes and sandals again, plus topical pullovers and hats. He grins at the contradiction of a statuesque pale mannequin with long blond hair wearing an *ao dai*. The shop's undersized entrepreneur stands nearby, scanning oncomers for a potential prospect. Marcel next passes a table of hand carved — it is hard for him to take that neatly printed sign seriously — figurines of faux stone, wood, and, as if to enhance the lie, plastic. A bland couple, twixies in matching shorts and hats, is admiring them, fondling them. He looks past the entry, inwardly urging the proprietor to cruise out and set the hook.

The novel adjacent configuration of a weathered striped tent, with a forlorn deck chair positioned under the fly, captures his attention. Again, he detects a heavy scent, but it's not of food and therefore not tempting. A foam-board sign aside the chair promises:

"Fortune Told! Mystery explain!! All QUESTION answer!!! THE REAL FUTURE reveal - - - $20."

The garbled tense doesn't detract from the boast. Actually, it adds vernacular emphasis, makes the promise more engaging. Yet, except for a square table draped in dark cloth, the dim oracular tabernacle appears to be empty. Marcel accelerates past, turning his head to look further into its interior for a brief, unrewarded moment.

"Only twenty," he observes aloud. "Worth a hundred."

Just beyond these sights, sounds, and smells, he comes upon a tight rank of vigorous young men, their white shirts rumpled, their cheeks ruddy from recent exertion. Hemming them in are a number of stalwarts in uniform. The five thus bracketed are neither subdued nor feigning contrition. They don't avert their eyes. On the contrary, they look confidently into the faces of the officers. The youth notably less disarrayed than his companions is gesturing with a large, black-bound volume. He points to it with the stiff open hand of a pedagogue. Policemen and onlookers appear equally attentive as he grasps the worn black book in both hands and raises it in front of him, its gilt edges catching the sun.

Satan's Holiday has been addressed. There's no need to hear the spokesperson's rationalization — supposedly enshrined in the proffered holy text — or the mild reproaches he and his comrades might be receiving. They aren't the fully mature, the twenty- and thirty-year olds who slink out from darkness to look for someone to blame. They are just past adolescence and acting out what they have been given, not what they are yet to grasp they have earned. They are youths in training, coarsely and safely practicing their nascent rage, and thus harbingers of a grimly familiar future. The thought makes Marcel shudder. He cannot hear either side of their debate, if that's what it is. He cannot know and he doesn't want to know the lesson being conveyed. He doesn't care to discern who truly is the giver and who the recipient. He can only guess from what he already fears is being proven correct. On this day, action has spoken and all soon will continue on their way. That's assured. It's already determined. The pro forma chastisement was made, and deemed necessary by current municipal rule, nothing more. Prohibitions and conventions change. Formal rules and laws change. Societies change. The more pressing question, therefore, is: Who will be the next assigned victims? What, beyond color, may soon become a definitive dividing line?

Old, alone, and suddenly chilled by the onshore breeze, Marcel turns to conclude his mid-afternoon walk, stopping for a moment in front of the custom shirt maker's window. Bright sunlight bounces off the white buildings behind him. He sees as much reflection as display but ignores the faintly familiar shape on the glass. Folded finished goods, each with a coordinated tie pushed under its collar, are on tiered stands. Mingling with these are the superimposed reflections of the street and storefronts behind him. A sudden motion in front of a recessed entry enlivens that static vista. Ample, well beyond being a girl, she has her arms out and slightly up. Even in profile, he can discern her warm welcoming. Marcel watches a tall figure approach and embrace her. They stand apart for a moment, then kiss and embrace again, for a few beats longer this time. The man puts his arm around her waist, guiding her back along the way he has come to her.

Marcel's eyes track along the glass front, following the couple in the partial mirror of the shop window until his view is blocked by a parked car. Momentarily displaced in time, his gaze retreats, is again straight ahead so as to study the known figure directly in front of him. The slant blaze of the afternoon sun seems to thin its hair. Shoulders rounded, arms hanging slack, a figure whose age is accentuated by highlighted wrinkles, it stares out at him. It appears shorter, more compact than he remembers or would like himself to be. He pulls his shoulders back and tries to add stature, endeavoring to reassert something of his real self. The image obeys. It's as real as the reflected images of the now departed couple.

His mouth in a firm line, Marcel grips his cap and extends his arm downward with it. He curls the fingers of his other hand into a light fist and braces it against his pant leg, thumb aligned with the seam. Satisfied, but yet not, he turns away from the shop window, crisply as he was once taught. Pacific is a few steps ahead; the bus stop is on Main, a few blocks farther on. The sun lower and now not as warming, he holds his cap stiffly at his side. He takes long, measured, weakly familiar military strides, his eyes tight and peering into the distance.

"Weevils, patiently waiting. Waiting for their time to emerge and infest.... Why are so many silent? Where has America gone?" he asks aloud without fear of being overheard. "Where is it going?"

STONE

The end of history is really a beginning.

STONE

Do not ask me again about the stone and its dark stains or of why I have it there, in that special place. I will tell you, but first I must tell you about me. I am not a talkman. So, while I cannot tell you everything or speak as well as they, only I can tell you everything about me. You have only recently come here. I began here. My past is here. Your past, the past of all of you who have come to visit, is elsewhere and I am certain you already know much of it. Now you need to know something of mine. I will speak truthfully. I must. You must know who I am. You must know who we are before your coming here can have a true reason. This is why I will share something of me with you.

I am sorry that I was shy and suspicious when the first of you came. You may have been among them on that day. I could not tell you apart then. There was so much that was strange to me. I was fearful. All of you were the same as we but so different from us, so unreal in many ways. That frightened me. That fear is gone. I can tell each of you from the other now. You have become different in understandable ways. You have become real that way. So I must be a voice to you, as a talkman is a voice to me. If I take too much time, please do not shake your head and start away. You will understand, once I am done. You will understand why I honor that stone and why it has blood upon it. Yes, blood. That is the nature of those stains.

Whose? I will tell you. But first, look there. You see the mountains far in the distance? When the air is clear, the sinking sun makes them bright with color. It can be beautiful to watch, if only for those few moments of the day ending. In the morning they reappear and the sun can paint their rugged bulk from another direction. So, if you are lucky, you can see their brief beauty two ways. I have not visited those peaks despite that they beckon. They are too far. It is too difficult a journey, even with animals that would carry for me, if the plan is to go and to return. The purity of being upon them as they are bathed in red and purple and gold, and of being bathed in the changing hues myself, would be a fine adventure. But there is no need. What I see I may see better from here than when upon them. Seeing them in the distance has always been enough.

Look before them. Do you see that dark slash that butchers the plain? It is a great canyon that is much closer than the mountains. I have been there and returned many times. The journey to its bottom is difficult, but I always had good reason. Later, I had need. The talkman tells of a river that once flowed between its steep sides. He tells of brown torrents that tore at men and their animals, that would carry them away to die if they were not alert. That must have been long ago, for I have never seen such rushing waters. Only trickles will be found there now, growing larger only in the proper season, when we have had rain. It is very dry and quiet otherwise.

The talkman speaks of much like that, of things and happenings and places that I cannot remember because I have never seen. It is not that he saw and remembers. He simply tells the tales. He simply teaches of the things and the happenings and the places of which he was told of and taught. There is no one with such memories of their own now. There are just the tales.

To go down into that dry canyon requires wits as well as need. You must not tumble or be hit by what tumbles from above. You must watch for holes that could break bones or hide large, creeping creatures that could bite and poison you. There are animals large enough to hunt you, which you must be alert for and avoid. Smaller evils are abundant and unforgiving as well. Above all, you must be able to find water. To carry enough for the journey there and back is not possible even in the best of times. It is very dry there, even more so than here. You must know the proper signs, which plants to cut and where to dig as you go, to find enough good water for yourself, and for your animal if one is with you. In the cool times, the small stream may be there but often is not, so you must prepare always. Some make loud plaints for favorable fortune on their trek and for the stream to be alive for them. Some take along potent charms. These may help, but knowing is better.

Here we have places for water that we can rely on, that are here for everyone. We make our homes near to these accustomed places. In the canyon you must often look anew. You must trust the signs will be there and that you will find them. You can live a long time without easy food. Life is short without water. Loud complaints and pleading and charms will not change that.

So, yes, I have been there, to the bottom of that canyon. I was helped by animals that carried without complaint and were as alert as I. Otherwise, I could not have gone. When I was young and alone, I followed the deep, twisting slash simply because I wanted to know. That was important then. To know. I went for great distances, always toward where the sun disappears, to find if it had an end. Each time I went a little farther because I could, because I could go faster. I had learned to know my way. I had wanted, I had hoped to see the bright arches that stand, as the talkman tells, where the canyon becomes tight, where its walls are close together and the sky is seen only through a narrow slit. Sadly, I never reached them.

When it was time to have a wife, I gave up such visions. There was much to do, much to prepare for, once I was no longer to be alone. The canyon became a place to go because of need not because of wish or simply to know. I went for its rounded stones, the kind that are found only there and that I needed to finish my house. It had to be a good house, a sturdy house, as I will tell you. I would have the woman only after it was ready for her. When it was done, she left her mother and her father and came to be with me. Then came children, and we were the mother and the father. Time passed quickly. There was much to do so that all would be safe and well fed. There was much to teach, as I had been taught. I made no more long, difficult journeys.

Too soon, it seemed, the children were gone. Then she, too, was gone, as I will tell you. I thought then about going back into that canyon. I was alone and there was time to seek out its mysteries. I still think to do that.

No, do not be concerned. It is only the wind and the dust. These bother my eyes sometimes.

The far canyon. Yes. I could have taken my animal and gone again. But, to go no farther than I had already gone and yet return? I had no need. Or to go and just keep going? Curiosity is not enough. If I were sure the canyon led to a better place, one less hot and less dry, then, yes, I might have ventured so far. The talkman tells of this. He promises a place beyond the canyon's narrows, where its walls separate and there is a broad open space that is always green. But such talk is not real until some have been there and return to tell of it as memory, as something of their own and not simply as repeated tales. Promises and tales are not enough. I am older and less able. I tire. And I again have someone here, the new one. Perhaps there will come that time when, were I to go, I would feel no reason to return. Then, true tale or not, able or not, tired or not, it would not matter. I would be ready. That itself would be a reason.

But not yet.

Yes, I would like to have seen with my own eyes those arches, those with the upright pillars the talkman speaks of. They span the cliffs, he has said, but are not part of them. Why they would be there, how they came to be, and if they still exist I cannot say. Perhaps you can and will share that with me. The talkman calls them the relics, the monuments described to him as always being there, as being there through all the seasons of sun and storms. I would like to have at least once approached close to them, to have seen their stark beauty for myself, their interwoven smooth lines and the gentle, womanly curves that the talkman describes as clearly as if he has seen them.

Mysterious relics can be found much nearer, on this side of the canyon. There are smooth, gray slabs that lie on the ground and can be approached easily. One is very close, at the base of that hill, not far from where once stood the home of my father. I can walk with you there, if you wish, if you have time. The slab is like a partially buried stone except that it is more even and flat and very large. Drifts of the soft sand move over it with the winds to bury then reveal parts of it. What can be seen has no end and makes it seem as if there is much more of it that remains hidden. It seems, also, that it, like the pillars and the arches, could not have been made by nature. It is too smooth, too even. And it is decorated with simple lines that have faded but seem to have had a purpose because they are so straight and so even.

Long ago, when our history began, so the talkman tells, the sheets were connected. They formed long, gray paths that sparkled and reflected the morning and evening suns, were like rippling water in afternoon heat. After a midday rain they glistened so to hurt the eyes. When the talkman describes these things, it seems these, too, he has truly seen, that he is remembering them from his own experience. That cannot be. No one has memories from so long ago. There are only the tales.

But I am not the one to tell you of these things. That is for the talkman. I can recite little of the far past. It has not for me to pass on the tales. Life has given me much to do, but not that. I am ignorant in that way. Yet, I am not stupid. I am smarter than many.

I see you smile. Perhaps you are right. I should not say that of myself. Still, it is true. I see what is around me and have made use of it better than many. Not everything has to be done in the same way as before. Not everything has to be as in the talkman's tales. Not everything has to be as he teaches. I have found, without having heard or being taught of, new ways to do things. And others have learned from me. May I say just one? I do not mind that you smile.

I once saw a bird fluttering low on the ground, but it was not broken. It was not dying as if hit by my throw, by good luck, or made sick, by bad. It was forcing the dry earth over and through its feathers. Why? I thought. Perhaps to clean itself? From that I thought to throw the very fine sand from the white hill — the one there, see? — into the pots of soap we make from the fire ash and cooked fat. It became much easier to clean things with such soap. The pots, hunting tools, myself. I was proud when others agreed and did the same. That was more than a recited tale. It was more than a memory.

I have imagined yet other new ways to be or to do. I say this to you not because I am proud. I say it because you need to understand that we here are not stupid people. Some things we just do not yet know. We are not bound to our past, only to our present so we do learn. But what we do not know sometimes frightens us. Is that so strange? Many fear visitors such as you, you see, because they do not know you. I did not know you at first, but now I do and do not fear you, merely find you mysterious. Even though you say you come from far away, what you speak of tells me you have a history with the same terrors as we. Therefore, I think that perhaps you are related to those the talkman speaks of, the distant people described so clearly in his tales.

Tell me, were there really those who long ago moved easily, without pause and faster than the fastest animal, along those hidden, flat stretches of stone that once extended from one great collection of people to another? I cannot imagine how such could be. Why would they work so hard to lay down those broad, dull ribbons for that? To speed along without stopping for sleep, or for food and water? What would be the need? In the tales are great crowds of them, who are said to have lived one next to the other, forever in each others' shadows. They built their homes one atop another, the talkman says. Was it for this that they needed to travel so far along those stony paths? Simply to be alone again?

These tales are strange. Still, as they were told and retold, the darkness amid rippling splashes of night fire allowed them to feel true. But when light would come and I would look over the sand and stubble of the rocky plain that extends to that canyon, then to the mountains beyond, and to the horizon in every direction, I could not understand how it could have been as the talkman tells. That there ever were so many of such people in one place or that they should have moved about so, seems very strange. Yet, the slabs, buried in the sand and scrabble, are there to stand upon. I had thought to some day follow them like spoor, to track from one exposed piece to another and see where they might lead. But, as with the distant reaches of the canyon and the startling color often bathing the mountains far beyond, such an adventure would take much effort, more than I could offer.

The exposed slabs and the distant arches are only a small part of the talkman's tales. It is with the great explosion that his tales always begin each new cycle. Only a fraction, the most fortunate of those long ago, are said to have survived that big event and all that followed, the many seasons of overlapping waves of heat, rains, and wind. Before, it had been a generous world for them, a world that offered more ease and abundance than one should plan for. There were large ripening fields, great masses of animals, houses of stone strong enough for them to be built very tall, each upon the other as I have said. It seems sad that the many types of plants, the many roaming animals, and the great collections of people were overcome. I can only marvel at the tales and try to imagine what sort of people they might have been, how they might have lived. It must have been sad for it to end.

Our history began far from any great collection of people with their ease, their abundance. We began here, scattered about on the plain. Those whom I honor the most, because of the talkman, always lived in lonely, hard places, far from those so packed close together, one upon the other. Our early people did not die from the horrible noise and fire. That was the fate of those far away and it was painful but quick. Our early people died because of the soft blankets of death, the talkman tells, that fell upon them. Choking fine dust, gray, brown, or black, according to the season and the wind, was mixed with poison. They died, as people must, but often slowly, growing pale, bloody, and shaking, as did their animals. When this passed, it became the times that were very wet, wet like you cannot imagine, or dry, dry like you see it now. It was hard to live, even without the dust falling from the sky. Winds and pounding rain would last for days. Storms would overcome all. They would overcome the plants, the animals, the houses, the people. Then would come long stretches of heat and of being unable to find water to drink or to give the animals and plants.

Those at the start of our history are therefore spoken of with sadness and, often, with anger. We long for them, wish to hear everything about them. But we know little, except that generation after generation they remained scattered and apart. They persisted through the dry and the wet, and we are here because of them. We understand that our strength flows from theirs. We have our history through them. How else would I be here? The talkman line formed the tales and passed them down, even to now, through the many sons and fathers who would follow them. They were very wise to do that. It gave significance to the favor of that wisdom, the favor of being able to hold memories and pass them on. How else would I know of these things?

STONE

The rains now are not feared. They are not the choking, wet heaviness from dirty clouds. They are not the tales' fearsome rains. The tall storms of dust are past. Now, this is a good place to be. Children come. Plants grow. Animals are born, serve their purpose, and are eaten. We do as we must, as we have heard and been taught. When this is not enough, we adapt and learn, as I explained to you. We struggle but our history continues. It is a curious thing that, even among all that early death, in the tales we hear of men of our history who lived for many cycles of seasons. Sixty, a hundred, two hundred times some experienced the same recurring patterns of weather and stars, of heat and rain. Perhaps it was they who formed the talkman line, because they gathered so much to pass on. That, again, is something that I do not understand. It is another mystery. I have experienced less than ten hands of such cycles since a child and I am already tired.

I am glad that you are attentive. When visitors such as you first came, they talked much and listened little. They came, as have you, in shiny boxes that made much wind. I must tell you that I am still glad when their noise stops and the dust about them settles. To see them step out that first time, to see that they were similar to us but content to be so close to that noise, was amazing. Yet, their strange ways and manner, their silly questions, were not welcome. They told us of change and of different ways to do but little of themselves.

STONE

Or perhaps they did, and I did not understand. And I could tell I was not always understood by them. They kept looking at their thin sheets of shiny metal as we talked, seemed to use these to help them speak with us. When they left, they made no offer to take us with them. I would not have gone, of course, because I did not like how they pointed down to rough stones and said, "This is who you are." That was odd for a living thing to say to another. Yes, I am sure we were equally strange to each other. Now, with you, it is better. Coming to know you has made it better.

To survive took as much effort after the visitors came as before, despite their smiles, their promises, and their many gifts. The smiles went with them, and the gifts were as strange as the promises. I put those aside, much as I gave little thought to the useless matters they spoke of, like what may have happened, what did happen, or what may again happen. It is enough to be. All is what is. If what they have said to us is true, then we will see it. I will see it.

Yes, I hear the noise of your boxes. I understand you must leave. But stay just a moment longer. This is the first time I have talked so freely to one of your nature. I need to finish my tale of me for you. Yes? Yes.

I had a wife and I had children, as I have told you. The children have gone as they had need to do. That is the way with children. My wife also is gone but well before she had need to. She was a good and pleasing woman. Yes, yes, very pleasing.

No. Stay. Do not be concerned. It is nothing but the blowing dust. It often gets into my eyes and stings. Just a moment more and I will be done, and you will understand.

We had a good house, which I built for her, as father had done before mother went to him, and so before I came to him from her. I was the first and I was taught well. I knew to put my house in a hollow on the sunrise side of a small hill, so that it would be cool even on the worst of days. And I knew to make it big enough for children. These soon came, as I and my brothers had come.

The walls of the house were of double stacked stone. Flat pieces are plentiful here, easy to bring back. Of course, you must use only those stones that make a sharp sound when struck, as my father had taught me. The stones that sound dull as wood soon break into crumbles and make poor walls. Even the easy rains that now come will destroy them. Straight branches held up the stones over the doorway and the window of my house. Smooth, long poles spanned wall to wall, to make the roof. Upon these I put broad, thin pieces of flat stone and earth packed with crushed scrub. Inside, between those I laid to make the floor, I put clean earth. I wet it and packed it well. It soon became hard and did not blow up with the wind. I dug the fire pit and lined it with the stones that would remain whole in the heat of a close fire. These were from deep in the canyon. Such proper. rounded stones are very rare here on the plain. But they are common in the canyon, you see, so I went there for them. That was my reason then. Within that pit I arranged smaller stones, also from the canyon, where she could set the pots. It was all as my father had done and had taught me to do.

She came when all was ready, as promised. It was good to be with her. We enjoyed each other in the night, in the calm. From her came several children. Sadly, the first wasted away, as the talkman, who saw something I could not, had said would happen. He never grew past my waist, was always thin and pale as if never in the sun. He could do little. His cloudy eyes were another burden.

"He will never see you," the talkman had said. "He will never help you. He will never pass you on. You must give him this."

I did as the talkman advised but the bitter tea from the small hard plant with no spines only made him sick. Each time he would lose what little he had eaten along with the warm drink. He quickly became weaker, too weak to live. We placed him far away, over there, in the fiercely dry place that we are wise to avoid. I have only the memory of him now. Other children came and grew strong. That was good. They gave us joy as well as much to do. When still young enough to think of different paths but old enough to make the journey, they went their own ways. Even the girl, toughened by her brothers, soon was ready. She found her equal and went to him. As I have said to you, that is how it is supposed to be. With their going, once again the woman and I were alone in the quiet of our talk, alone in the sounds of the night and of our being together. From the first that she came to me, I had been content. Then, alone once again, we enjoyed each other as we pleased. Our days were simple.

When I was on top of her and I disappeared, she disappeared as well. That, too, was good and how it should be. Only, it was that way less often after her noise came. It arrived during a harvest. At first it was slight. It only made her pause. Then it grew loud and took over her as the months passed. It interrupted her as she talked, sometimes so that there was no voice for her words, only air. When I felt her tighten beneath me with the noise, being together in the night was not the same. The remedies of the talkman changed nothing.

After the season turned we placed our mat close below the window to feel the wind. She seemed to need its chill and at the same time to be pained by it. When I wanted to be with her, we lay on our sides. She on her right, I on my left. I could no longer lay on top of her, together in the night, in the darkness and quiet of our house. Moving into her was still moist and pleasant, but the noise grew and became overpowering. I still disappeared. She seldom did. I made most of the motion and then would rest. I could be quiet except for the rush of breath through my mouth and nose. She was still but could not be quiet. Her breaths came in sharp gasps. The noise flew out from her in heavy bursts, often with no pause. That was the price of holding it back until I had disappeared. She was a good wife.

While much had been dried and stored away, I had still to provide. I could not stay with her throughout the day. Sadly, I was glad for the time that I was away from the noise, even though I yet thought of it all the while and of how it must be when I was not there. When I would return, the sound of it would greet me from a distance. Soon it came that I could expect no sounds of meal making. No longer did I hear, ahead in the distance, the soft whoosh of a mat being shaken, the crunchy thump of her heavy stick against grain, or the crack of wood being broken for the fire. These came for me to do. Only when I set a pot on the stones that surrounded the fire and sat close to her did our house fill with the scent of herbs and meat. I cooked well, yet she ate little. She became thin, so thin I thought she could break. I tried to be careful with her. I did not let her do anything that required much strength. It was easy for me to do what once were her tasks and had become mine. We still had the night. I would lie on my left side then move into her so gently.

I knew. Yes, I knew the sharp noise was very bad. When the blood came, it was worse than the noise, worse than her tearing eyes and dark, tight face, worse than her thinned arms. It was bright and wet. It smelled hot and sweet, like from a goat when we celebrated the day of a birth or of a death or of a boy changing to a man. The talkman offered nothing. My insides moved and tingled with the fear that came with helpless watching. Her sharp noise would not stop and left bright, small specks on the back of her hand. She did not want to make wet stains on the stone of our floor or its earth, but the red dripped too easily from her when the noise shook her. She could not stop it. She could not make it wait. Small patches of it would grow dark beneath our feet.

No longer were we together as woman and man. I did not mind. Being close beside her was enough. Only, it was sad to see her hot eyes stare up through the smoke hole at a sky full of cold points of light. They would overflow as she fought hard against the noise, squeezed it back until it exploded from her. I would point to the bright sliver of moon, to the many tiny stars. It is a beautiful night, I would say to her, looking up with eyes that also burned. She would move her head slowly to say yes but I knew it meant no. How could it then be beautiful for her?

The blood came in a heavy flow on a bright afternoon of a fresh season. Head bent low and waiting for my return, she was leaning against the doorway of our house. Then she was not. I was not close enough to stop her slow sit, her silent descent onto the red warmth by the doorway. I ran to her. She was very still. She stayed very still. There was no noise. There was no sound but for mine.

When I told those first visitors of this, they looked at each other. I remember the way they looked at me and then again at each other, how this made me think that such never happens in their lives. They moved to touch me, but I moved away. Perhaps you were among them and saw. I am sorry, then, if I offended you. But I did not want to be touched, as I knew there really was no desire to touch me. They said they would help. They said they could make me a new house in another place.

"Will it be the same?" I asked them.

"Yes, of course," one said. "And it'll be better as well."

Since leaving my father I had lived in no other house than the one I built just as he had built his. Mine had the same strong stone walls, the same floor, the same window, the same door, and the same roof with the opening above the fire pit for the smoke. It was of me, by me. It was truly mine. Still, I replied that I would have their new house. Perhaps it would help me to forget.

But this new house is not at all like my old. It is cold and bare, as you can see. It is without meaning and shows no sign of having been made by someone who had a true and proper reason. The walls are smooth and too bright in the day. There is a window but it is not open as before, unless I do as they showed me. There is neither a fire spot nor a hole for the smoke, so there is no sky. There is no floor. There is only the same pale, cold, and bare hardness as of the walls. There is not a single stone in it. It is supposed to be a better house, yet, I am troubled by the redness that appeared at the edges of the doorway and around the inside of the window after the first big rain. The stains surround the ends of exposed metal, as if the house is itself bleeding from them. I can show you but I cannot look at them. They make my eyes burn.

A new wife, the talkman told me, would be a good thing for the new house. I thought the same. I did miss the disappearing and felt the truth of what he said. But, before that could be, it came to me that I needed to prepare. It came to me that I needed a special stone and something long and flexible from which to hang it. I wandered about for many days, casting my eyes down as I walked, searching. I did not look at the sky nor even think of it. I did not look into the distance. I did not look into faces. I looked only down, for the stone that was not usually of this place yet perhaps would free me from my past.

I found the simple twisted hide first and knew it would serve. Short, braided, and smooth along its length, its ends were rough where it had broken away from the animal that it once held fast. I soaked it for an entire day, until it became soft enough for me to undo the braid of three narrow strips of skin. I found the stone on another day, just as a hot sun was setting. The shadow of it helped. It pointed up and was just what I sought. It was shaped like an egg from a bird, but gray, dark gray like sky before strong rain. I bounced the smooth stone in my hand and was satisfied. I needed exactly this stone, you see, one from here and therefore rare, not one from the canyon where there were many.

I washed again the strands of hide that evening and left them in the water to soften. There was little sleep for me because my task had truly only begun. I watched the sky go from black to dull gray, watched the short burst of promising color from a rising sun. I felt the strands and knew they were flexible enough to be tied together to make a single long strip, a thong. I wound its end around and around the stone, across itself and overlapping so that it would be secure. I tied it twice over, to be sure, leaving free just enough to go twice around my fist.

The stick was ready. I had sharpened and hardened its tip in fire many days before. I held it fast and pushed the pointed end through my lip, here, just above where a thin leaf of flesh binds it to the gum below my biting teeth. The pain was sharp, like the stick itself. A red drop appeared on the floor beside me. Then another and another. Seeing the red spatter, the small dots upon the dull sameness of that floor, I thought of my old house, our old house. This blood, I said then to myself, will bring an end to that. This blood, rich and fresh, was mine. It will erase the blood that was not mine, the blood of my memories.

STONE

The stick became slippery. It was hard to grasp it and twist it out from the fleshy hole. When it was free I had to sit quietly for a moment. I leaned the stick against my leg. With the bound stone upon my thigh, I began to thread the free end of the thong through the wound. But the hide was wet and limp. It would not pass through the hole, which grew smaller as the flesh swelled. I had to rest again from the pain. As I rocked in place, I felt the stick clinging to the hairs of my leg. It was still wet but drying, so I could not rest long. It came to me to fold the end of the thong over its point, now stained dark red. Bending double like a young man, and with the bound stone still safe on my knee, I pushed through the stick that carried the fold of softened hide. That was very difficult. There was much pain, a fuller pain, a pain duller, deeper, and more demanding than before. It was not easy and not kind. The red drops on my crossed legs mingled with clear drops from my eyes. But these were all small and of me, again of little importance. I knew then that not being easy and not being kind also were necessary.

When it was done, I bent forward close to the stone. I looped the end of the slippery thong over my lip and tied it, firmly but not so tight as to pinch. When I straightened, the stone hung against the hollow space between my small nipples. The length of the simple loop of hide was just enough. All of it was enough.

STONE

My lip sagged with the weight of it and eventually became dry as the days passed. The gum below my biting teeth also dried. The dryness of that which had always been wet and never noticed, the unfamiliar effort of the muscles of my jaw to keep my teeth just so, the feel of the air upon them — all of it was as I had expected. All of it was as needed to be. I had not seen this done and no talkman had told me to do so. That I knew what was needed came from within myself.

Soon the hot redness of the wound faded. I could eat and drink more easily. After many days the edges of the hole sealed over and became a darker shade of pink. I seldom ran because then I had to hold the stone and this was wrong. The stone needed to hang free in order make new memory. It was to teach me, as might the tale of a talkman. My jaw muscles became set and firm. I breathed only through my nose. I ate and drank slowly. I paid little attention to the looks from others, which grew less frequent because they, too, came to understand. I stayed away from visitors, like you, as well. What could I tell them that they would understand?

Only after the many weeks of healing did I let the talkman show me the new woman. I was surprised. She seemed very young to come to my house. I saw my daughter in her. But she agreed to be my new wife, as I wanted and the talkman said I had should have. I had missed looking at the night with someone. I wanted again to disappear. It was time for me. She had no one and it was time for her as well, the talkman said. Only, she wanted me to enter her from behind, like the wild and the kept animals I had watched as a boy and wondered at. I like to think that this was not because of the stone. She seemed to accept it as she did me. It bounced gently against her back as I pressed against her. As I held her breasts and disappeared she often seemed to disappear as well, but I was not certain. Still, it was good to be with her in the darkness.

This was our way until the crows came again. The large black birds were very loud and not pleasant to hear. They were attracted by the new growth and so, because of this, their coming was both good and bad. Standing in the opening of this, my new house, I watched a pair of them fly toward the nearby patch of shallow water. Night was coming. It was their time to drink and then rest. I understood their desire. I thought of their simple routine, much like mine. As I followed the silent pair, the harsh call of a lone crow, in that closest tree, startled me.

Faster than thought my head turned up and jerked toward the big bird that perched dull black and motionless against a pale sky. This sudden movement was too much for the flesh of my lip. It had been pulled down by the stone. It, too, had thinned. The loop of hide, now dry, its edges sharp, pulled through it. This produced a pain like from fire. The sudden wetness on my gums and my biting teeth was a great change. Drops of blood disturbed the dust at my feet. I looked at them and remembered many things, but as tales, not memory. Enough time had passed. I no longer had thoughts of why I needed the stone. All had become tales. Even the sharp noise of the crow had no meaning. The blood soon stopped and it was done. There was no need to shed tears.

You are kind to listen to me tell of myself. I feel you do mean well. Yes, this new house is safe from the wind and rain, as was promised. But it is so cold and so bare. See there? There is no smoke hole in the roof. The window, set so high in the wall, is sometimes open but is not covered with a weaving that will keep out small things yet let in the air. And my lip has healed, as you can see. The jagged tear has closed upon itself. Yes, I have kept the stone, but I have not put it there to instruct me. It is there to release me. I am no longer bound to it or to the past. Perhaps now it will be easier to listen to what you and the other visitors wish to tell me. I am ready to listen, when next you come. These may be good things, your coming as well as what you have to tell me. My future is short. I know that now. But I will listen.

RETURN FROM WILDERNESS

"Who knows what evil lurks in the hearts of men?"

RETURN FROM WILDERNESS

They were again at the edge of the tree line, well above their small rural town. Quiet, solely theirs on early mornings, it often seemed a lifetime away when they were endeavoring to restock their freezer. His father motioned to the crumpled young buck and nodded approvingly. Eyes wide open, its neck flexed, it looked ready to leap up and charge off, something to be followed for its last hundred yards or so of slow death. Except that those black orbs were already unseeing. Wisps of steam rose in the crisp, cold air from the blood pooling at its forelegs.

The middle-aged man stood downslope, slightly below his son, facing him and away from the sun just beginning to touch the ridge across the nearby narrow wash. His smile conveyed approval and a touch of congratulation, a hint of secondhand pride. The lad smiled back. It was his buck this time. Small and unwise compared to the fleet others of previous hunts, it was enough for his first success as well as for their needs.

The large wound that blossomed from the lower portion of his father's chest appeared suddenly, as if by magic. Down and feathers from his partially zipped parka mingled with an explosion of mist, its crimson mixed with beige. His father's eyes remained fixed upon him right up to the moment he fell back, legs and arms outstretched, his nostrils dark and flaring. His snow boots seemed outsized in that perspective but grew smaller in his son's eyes as a red stain formed on either side.

The lad looked to the motionless young deer, as if to find there a reason, an explanation, a comparison, a judgment. Overwhelmed by profound silence, it was several seconds, an unmeasured instant that hung on for an eternity in his remembrance of it, before there came a loud retort and the fading rumbling that followed. He ran past the carcass they had been about to gut and dismember. Violently pitched into another world, he unwisely let his rifle slip from his hands, something his father had often told him to guard against. He slumped heavily to his knees in the snow but didn't feel its cold reality, even through thin, nearly outgrown jeans.

He found it hard to tell the officers exactly what had happened. The truth was that he didn't know, couldn't really fathom what had taken place. It was far from anything he had or had expected to experience. His father may have seen such deaths but had never shared that, never related grim details from his military service. It was to be nearly a decade before the boy would have comparable experiences, of which he also never had occasion to speak but for a different reason.

RETURN FROM WILDERNESS

Showing promise of becoming so much like his father, robust in build and manner, he nevertheless felt like a subdued child while being interrogated. He could only repeat the same few lines from what seemed like a nightmare inspired by some late evening's tale but was not. The sheriff, however, was less concerned with him or investigation than with documentation. The boy had grown used to that form of oblique official interaction in his singular sorties into town. He had learned at an early age how to endure it. His father's advice had been simply stated on numerous occasions: "Stay out of their way and mind your own business."

But that become impossible on that and subsequent days.

He spent days in a cold, barred room before what was evident, those bare facts innocent of complication, were accepted. His rifle had been fired only once since its last cleaning, as he had told them, and as the clip and dead animal indicated. His father's, found leaning against the tree from which they had intended to hang and bleed the deer, had been as clean and redolent only of oil as on the evening before, when they were getting ready for that third, that last hunt of the season. The fatal bullet, pieces of which the coroner preserved despite contrary advice, left little doubt that it had issued from a rifle with a caliber and configuration far different from either of theirs. And it had come from a great distance, according to any rational interpretation of the adolescent's statement. Yet, despite all of this and the nature of the wound itself, they had attempted to implicate his or his father's rifle in the death, calling up the possibility of anger or negligence despite scant evidence for either. Anything was possible, they seemed to judge, and nothing was to be discounted. That was understandable. If otherwise, then the blame would have needed to fall upon one of their own.

Slightly stooped now, he stands silent, reviving the echoes of that formative past. Much of what he has tried to remember he cannot. All of which he has tried to forget he could not. On this day, fifty-five years later, the clearing in which he stands comes alive with the full force of a distant but never lost reality. Everything is green and the ground is bare of snow. The low growth is nonspecific yet familiar. The open space seems smaller, more constricted than he anticipated, but at its core their once designated special spot is unchanged. The simple act of being there allows memories to emerge from hiding in defiance of time. Yes, he muses, there is the same tree, its odd shape tolling in his eyes much as a steeple bell would awaken his ears. Its uniquely misshapen limb is as thick and as seemingly sturdy as before, only higher up on the trunk, he judges, too high now to serve its once intended purpose. The lonely boulder with its uppermost aspect flat, as if sliced from some large body of gneiss, is unmoved, unmoveable. It had been their stony table. Today it is the most reliable marker. He runs his bare hand over its surface, which is not quite level but flat enough to serve. He traces the wavy patterning, imagining fresh blood, dark stain, and where he had set his pack and sheath knife on that day.

Why did I return? he asks of himself. He knows the one responsible for that single shot, a boy about as old and able as was he, is probably gone. He knows who boasted he could do it at five hundred yards, perhaps one thousand. Not yet an independent man and imprudent, the young man's act was no doubt excusable in the eyes of many, much as it was celebrated in the minds of some. Sickness, accident, age, or infirmity has, singly or in concert, most likely wreaked the revenge he was due. But those are paltry allies. He can derive no satisfaction from what may have already overcome the more lucky than skilled assassin because he would have played no part in it.

"Probably gone now," he says aloud, which is less than a certainty but more likely than what he wanted. He would prefer that he be needfully infirm, sickly and suffering, longing for death and denied it. That was his unresolvable hope, until now. Now, presumption isn't, can't be enough. He seeks verification, certainty.

He turns and looks downslope, toward the town. It has grown substantially, which is surprising considering how little there is elsewhere in this region, how paltry has been what modern commerce and industry could draw from it. From his present high vantage point it seems to have a far larger extent than that which he pulls from imperfect memory. He tries to overlay the present and the past, tries to make a clear comparison, but he cannot bring both simultaneously into focus. He lowers his gaze to scan the wooded terrain leading down. The steep and rocky creek is noisy with snowmelt. It was more treacherous to cross this time, which impressed him since he hardly ever noticed it when trekking up this far with his father. The entire climb was hard, in fact. More than once he thought to abandon it. He's glad he didn't. The way down will be easier for many reasons, not the least of which being that he achieved his interim goal.

That slight rise beyond the wash in the near distance, that offending rise, that terrible rise, has retained its tight stand of tall pines, the sturdy straight trunks against which to lean, take careful aim, then to have disappeared among. Boastful, youthful coward, he thinks, instantiating the calumnies of other, secretive mature cowards. He recalls the stinging viciousness that survived then because it wasn't confronted, because it fulfilled perceived, stoked needs, viciousness that survives still, because it is submerged and provides some measure of strength to the otherwise weak.

Pivoting sharply, he puts his back to the town and the distant stand of trees. Yes, he thinks, blinking away uncontrollable shards of memory, a thousand yards. Three seconds for the sound to reach this spot.... Only a single second for the bullet.... The two second latency of eternity.

Blank-faced before the gray stone veined with white, their butchering stone, he takes out an envelope, which is yellowing along its glued seams, from the inside pocket of his overcoat. The clipping, so carefully preserved within, is brittle. It's the cheap news print of the local weekly of those times. Again, as on many recent occasions, he must be careful when unfolding it. He cants his head and slips on his readers with his free hand. Yes, his name is also there, in the paragraph following the description of the death of his father. Further down is a listing of others suspected but, means being discounted and citing judicial insufficiency, promptly declared not culpable by the local authorities. The name that should be there is absent.

Threats and feints, it seemed, are never sufficient as proof. But, federal agents had later claimed, they were indicative. They therefore had mounted an investigation, which opened wounds but resolved nothing. The suitable and most likely weapon, something military such as was known to have been owned by the father of one of the town's young men, the one that taunted him, was never found. Witnesses, before or after the fact, likewise could never be located. Only denials came forth, never confessions; not even those implicit or inferred. Life is a right. To take it is a crime. Why did that need to be construed as such a novel idea, an idea perhaps not applicable in his father's case? More to lose than to gain by pursuing it further became the common and eventually accepted view. For all, that is, except him. He looks down at the fragile clipping. That preliminary news report is all he has, since he had gone to live with his aunt very soon after his father's death. Less palpable but more real, he has what came before, what he had been subjected to in town and by whom, and what his father had told him.

He adjusts his glasses to read aloud the names of those questioned, names that are familiar to him even then because his father had spoken of them, had pointed them out from a distance. Quietly but earnestly, he had been instructed to be careful were he in town alone, to avoid them because what they would not do to a man in public they had no fear of imposing upon a boy. Denigration is their tool, he had said. Reaction is their excuse and "... weakness is their opportunity. So keep away from 'em and don't answer back."

Most, perhaps all of them are gone now, he again considers. People don't have such long lives in the mountain wilderness. Their riddance would seem a net good, but he would have gained little from being its agent. Any change thereby would have been for the worst. The simple fact is that abundant affiliations of hate exist and fester because of insufficient resources. They will always do so because there are always those at the bottom seeking reasons.

RETURN FROM WILDERNESS

Yes, time itself, in its simple progression, has accomplished much of what he had then and thereafter wished for but could not undertake. Just as well, he thinks. A quick death would never have imposed upon them the arbitrary and unjustified pain that he had been forced to experience. Grimaced lingering would suffice, but was then and still is beyond his ability to impose. The pain of innocents is more practical, would provide better recompense. He tilts the yellow sheet toward the low sun. From each name he reads he knows there must have come a line of loved ones. From the unnamed one as well. There must be wives, children, nephews, nieces. And grandchildren, no doubt, since it has been long enough. There must be many of theirs alive who can yet feel pain, even though they, the most proximate guilty party and his abettors, no longer matter. He needs only to search them out, to make casual inquiries that would not alarm. His distinctive facial features and skin tone will not draw stares as once they had. These might not even elicit covert reactions, or at least, no more so than a strange manner of speaking or a haircut that resembles nothing their barbers would attempt. But deep inside, those below are likely to be the same. Times change. People, not so much.

After checking the breech, as he was long ago taught to do, he places the rifle upon the worn case he has stretched out on the butchering stone. He never thought to discharge it since that day, even though it's a much finer piece than was his own ancient, long gone Remington. Kept safe and secure, he would take it out only rarely, for oiling and cleaning, which he now sees were inadequate. His finger comes away stained a pale red after he rubs it along the receiver. He rubs harder and senses the grit, the pocks. He shakes his head at his neglect, his failure to respect. His father would be angry, he thinks.

"Silly. This whole thing is pointless," he says down to the weapon with little conviction.

He has never hunted since that day and does not remember what happened to his own rifle. Perhaps he left it here, on the mountain that day, or left it behind when he went to his aunt's, or sold it to a thrift shop. It was simply absent, gone, as were the memories supposed to be. He kept his father's hunting weapon, since it was the only thing of substance that he would have of him. When first contemplating this final trip, his intention, however, was to leave it at the fatal spot and finally be rid of it, to be rid of all of it. He might, at the same time, create a memorial to his father, if only tenuous and in his own mind. The thought took years to become firm intent. Even now, he is trying to decide.

He never married. He has no children, of course, and very few friends. His life since that singular day has been one of isolation, despite that he came to be educated, had a profession, and made a good living. Being close to others was never comfortable for him. Profoundly conflicted, he preferred noncommittal solitude and superficial association. He preferred to be free of any need for explanations, revelations, or talk of personal history. Over the years this became itself a burden, something he wished he had not allowed to take over him. Perhaps, he recently came to think, if he discarded that respected firearm of his father's, that anti-talisman, he would be freed from its associated past and could learn to enjoy people. It wouldn't be too late. Perhaps, he reasoned, he could expurgate all of the linked, periodically reinforced anger were he to come one last time into this wilderness of remembrance and leave it.

He could lean it against their special tree, he now poses, but that would not serve. It simply would be found and serve another. Better would be to bury it at the spot where his father fell, which spot is indelibly fixed in his mind. He knows he could pick it out with as much certainty as if there were already a marker. But he cannot bring himself to try. Nor has he brought the means to do so. Painfully aware of his irresolution, he fixes his gaze on the old but ageless bolt action Browning 30-06. He smiles when the identification comes so firmly to mind.

The light is fading. He had started out before noon, but later than he intended and with less strength in his legs than he expected. He shakes his head, once again unsure of the real reason or reasons why he has exerted the effort to climb the trail in these final hours, if, in fact, that is what they are destined to be. He turns to look down at the town. Lights have come on along many of its streets. There is a scattering of cars following yellow cones. He stares and attempts to spot the once familiar intersection with its blinking, then singular traffic light. There, he thinks. Is that it? If so the café and market should be right there. He had visited both with his father. There had originated the reasons for the warnings from him. The suppressed feelings of being dismissed, disrespected, and stared are released once again. When he was alone and vulnerable, which emboldened them, worse had come. His brow furrows with the recollections.

"Did ya read in the paper what they did down in Georgia to anotha one of ya?" a familiar tormentor, the father of the one he saw on the rise that day, had asked while laughing. He then fake-gagged with his hand at his own throat. He snorted a final chuckle. "Ya can read okay, can't ya, boy?" he had asked.

"Leave him alone," another said. "He's only a kid."

"Yeah. But they grow up.... Ya goin' to be a strong nigger, like yar pop, boy? Take more of ours wha's out there for ya sef?"

With that he had waved up at the mountain with its trees and made another choking sound.

It's easy to frighten a youngster, a schoolboy. The courage for it is not hard to muster. It can amuse as well as elevate.

RETURN FROM WILDERNESS

He has seen both faces so many times in his sleep. At worst the coarse man was merely the instigator, but he's as guilty as the boastful youth who stood aside one of the pine trees and nestled the barrel of the heavy sniper rifle against it at the base of a low branch. Many must have issued from that line. Many were and perhaps still are close to them, even though they, those directly a part of it, may be gone. His pain changed him forever. Why should not they, those still extant, sample it? Why should they not share it on behalf of the many others? True, the spawn are innocent of any evil against him, except for what they no doubt harbor privately now and rarely share. Yet, he had been innocent then. Innocent and weak. His innocence counted for nothing but his weakness made him vulnerable. Now, for them, so does having something to lose. For him the inverse rings true: Having nothing to lose is liberating.

This is what he has been thinking about.

From that day to this he has never fired his father's fine Browning. While periodically cleaning it and remembering, he had never even looked through its telescopic sight. When he lifts it now to do so, he is dismayed to see how cloudy the image is. Discoloration has bled into the periphery of the optics and the cross hairs are distressed. It would no longer serve its intended purpose. But that is immaterial. He would stand close enough for it not to matter. He would not need to brace it to aim.

RETURN FROM WILDERNESS

The sudden clarity of that thought, the complete image that it evokes startles him. It may be that within that thought are the means to banish the amplified memories that have kept him awake and disturbed his days in these, his final years. That he, out of all, is alone and has always expected little should make that easier.

He puts the rifle down gently, fingering the bulge in the case that signifies the clip and several loose cartridges are in their proper place. Although he has declined as he aged, these rounds certainly have not. They never do. Without specific effort or plan they are always ready for their designated task. He, on the other hand, had to be made ready, had to be made willing.

The case accepts the rifle easily. He grasps the worn leather handles and notes its balanced weight. With a final look downslope, retraces his steps along the well-worn trail. Many have benefited from what they could glean from these hills, lakes, and forests. Many will again. But he will hunt elsewhere. He will come down from the mountain, at last to return from wilderness. He looks at his watch without having any real need. The dimming sky itself allows tomorrow to be soon enough.

MEMORY

The disorientation of what was confuting what is.

MEMORY

There was no need for Rick Blaine to have died that way. Sure, I know. That's Hollywood. It's what they do. It was entertaining, as usual, but somehow different. *Casablanca* just didn't feel the same, not on that recent viewing at any rate. I really wanted a different ending.

I've a long list of favorite films, most of them from years ago. While the details of some may have faded, I can mentally replay the highlights, the iconic scenes of nearly all. When sleep is difficult, I'll replay these to subdue the intrusive thoughts. Films recently or repeatedly seen can be more easily revived. I might start with an exceptionally good opening hook and hopscotch through an entirety. The disorderly pieces of a whole, its barely scripted incidentals, usually suffice. Recollection fills in the gaps, takes the place of cinematic priors and thereafters.

But I prefer the old, the well known, over the new, the recently judged. Motes seem to survive even though immersed in banality. "You know how to whistle, don't you, Steve? You just put your lips together and … blow." I'll never forget, nor fail to mimic on the proper occasion, that promise to "... be bahk." I'll forever smile at the thought of the Fat Man's incongruously brisk stride in *The Maltese Falcon*. In its concluding scenes his paunchy disappointment at the reveal of the false bird is undeniable, his maniacal, slashing descent from expectation into despair explicable, his final transfiguration to reinvigorated optimist plausible. Of an entirely different genre is the lilting "Daisy, Daisy, give me your ..." with HAL's slowing, distorted bass playing against the rhythmic hiss of a human's constrained breathing. Or go back, far back, to the mask ripped away, the classic shock without shriek. Silent surprise worked well then; it's too simple a fright for most now.

Awakened emotive connections underlie the power of narrative based upon moving images and coordinated sound. From a properly constructed sequence we experience serenity or fright, joy or envy, elation or sadness. "Hello, you old Savings and Loan!" in *It's a Wonderful Life* conjures up sympathetic relief during any Christmas week; the tinkling of a small bell in its finale is sufficient to elicit misty eyes. After any good horror film we may attribute dark significance to a door's or floorboard's creak, to footsteps behind. No matter what the style of production, the point of a film is to convey a meaningful, even if understood to be false, reality.

I know. It's regressive to persist in using the word "film" in this world of bits and bytes. Old habit, I suppose.

For a cinematographer, being "e"ffective is primary. Illusion is the key to unlocking connection. The proper aim, however, is to be "a"ffective, to elicit emotional connection beyond mere faithful representation, beyond meaning and conventional reality, beyond words and formal truths. Via images on a screen or words on a page or space-occupying art, the skillful do move us beyond simple recall and raw appreciation of facts. Those with lesser skills depend upon explication. Their works offer only brief relevance or fail totally despite, or possibly precisely because of detailed annotation. The best succeed without it. The intellectual insights their works evoke follow rather than lead, are incidental rather than revelatory, responses to rather than causes of. Significance, I mean to say, should be a consequence of the emotions aroused, not their cause. Some artists have an instinct for attaining it regularly. Others stumble onto good fortune, create an isolated success that their subsequent work reveals would've been wiser to have let remain so.

Right?

But that's another matter, the craft of media professionals. It's my own altered affective response that I'm struggling to understand. Some of my favorite films feel different, their emotional impacts seem altered. I find this troubling since, as much as these could be signs of personal growth, so could they be symptoms of regression. I can accept the fading of remembrance. I'm old enough. Still, I'm of the opinion that affect, if retrievable, if evocable at all, should not change. Yet, some familiar plots have come to lack the expected, previously satisfactory thematic arcs.

A good example is the film *Casablanca* or, I should say, my reaction to it. As many times as I've watched that piece of cinematic escapism, that mildly propagandistic story of clear-cut heroes and villains, it always had elicited feelings of adventures well-met and yet to come. This last time, just last week, it didn't. The ending struck me as cold, didactic, devoid of promise. It was appropriate to the plot and internally consistent but, at the same time, teasingly unsettling. It left an itch of unsatisfied connection. My reaction to *Casablanca's* resolution was, and remains, as much disturbing as unexpected.

The consummation of *Casablanca* is, of course, that melodramatic quintet at the airport. First Rick Blaine and Captain Renault, then Ilsa and Victor Laszlo arrive, each anxiously anticipating the departure of the Lisbon plane. Major Strasser is en route, thanks to Renault's casual duplicity, only they don't know that. Tight shots of the iconic German officer in an open car are cut in to make evident his anxious determination. On the tarmac in front of the hanger, Renault does Rick's forceful bidding. Ilsa resists. She can't accept that he is sending her off with Laszlo.

"But, Richard, no, I, I –" she says.

Yes, they'll always have Paris. The close-up of her upturned face, the moist eyes and faintly parted, pouty lips, worked its magic on me. I was unabashedly moved. I took a deep breath, as always. As Ilsa and Victor blend into the mist, I felt glad for them.

Were *Casablanca* to be made today, some tedious, over-hyped hack would no doubt insert a song, probably entitled "Last Plane to Lisbon," using ascending chords and a terminal minor, thereby asserting the device of plot emphasis but primarily striving for secondary residuals.

Hah!

Anyway, leaping from his car, Strasser confronts the pliant Renault and the resolute Rick, who are gazing into the milky mist. When informed that "Victor Laszlo is on that plane," he marches to a phone box with briskly projected, evil intent. He's sharply defined, monadic. He grabs the cumbersome handset.

"Put that phone down!" Rick growls.

"Get me the radio tower," Strasser demands, his expression a rigid mask of rage. His hand explores his coat with obvious intent.

There's another unheeded command from Rick. "Put it down!" he says, with his so distinctive intonation.

Rick's pistol is at the ready. Strasser's Luger is a hastily retrieved blur, but unmistakable. That quintessential Nazi sidearm was a staple of the Us versus Them films of that era. They both fire. Strasser's trigger pull is quicker, his aim surer. We don't see Rick take the bullet, but we hear it and hear him fall. We hear also the clatter of his gun on the tarmac.

I've seen Bogart die in other movies and so could imagine his toothy grimace. Rick uncharacteristically hesitated. He considered options. Strasser did neither. From behind, his slight jerk then, for a frontal frame or two, the brief shock reflected by momentarily closed eyes suggest a superficial wound. Not so for poor Rick. Strasser's shot, even while barely aimed, is fatal.

I appreciate the entertainment value of secondhand reification, the re-experienced impact of that which is itself a fiction. It's what keeps classics in circulation. Being taken back to a known moment, whether it be real or fictional, can be rejuvenating, reassuring, well worth forsaking novelty. Eidetic imagery can take us farther in. Yet even that only partially travels the road to full veracity. Remembering, viewing a media image of, or internally recreating a representation of place or thing or event, no matter to what extreme of faithful detail, is notably different from experiencing it again. That requires a coordinated replay of emotional context, one based upon a complex internal state that may never have existed otherwise and, confounding many attempts to recreate it, is probably different in each of those impressed by otherwise identical externals. We aren't, after all, simply sensor-driven machines. No barrage of visual and auditory input will recreate reality unless it awakens latent, native, and, most often, individualistic emotions.

Psychologists have suggested that olfaction, a most primitive sense, is powerfully endowed in this way. As a neurobiologist I can certainly agree with that. Even in the highly developed sapient brain, the sense of smell has retained its archaic anatomical connection to the cerebral circuitry controlling drive and the urges that we experience as emotion. Odors can bind to events, to specific places and times, thereafter sufficient to reawaken their emotional contexts. We've all experienced this, I'm sure. The spicy scent of a hand-thrown pizza, for example, can transport me back decades, a half-century or more. Sometimes this is to a summer evening, standing alone, watching an expanding circle of dough being tossed. Or I may be momentarily on the bench backseat of a car by the reservoir, with the open, flat box warm across our thighs. Perfumers are adept at using the nose. The olfactory sense could someday provide the key to solidifying the truth of an emergent world.

Right?

Films and videos lack that, obviously. Surrogate representations via current media necessarily rely upon cleverly crafted audio and images. While the latter may be primary, a well designed sound track — with rich instrumentation, with clever chord progression and modulation of pace — can pull us further in. But it won't guarantee we'll be full participants. To suspend the awareness of artifice, to truly feel a moment as fact not as recreation, there must be more. All of our senses, of course, contribute to the creation of our private realities. An odor would serve, as I've said, or perhaps so would making use of an articulated chair. If its motion is coordinated with the images, it only has to shift in small increments to make a person as dizzy, to give the same white knuckles and nausea as from a real midway ride. That's feasible right now and much more practical for home use than is olfaction.

We should never underestimate how much people will spend to reify their fantasies or how much time they will devote to doing so. There's a lot of money made from servicing that desire. Technology has merely added the means, the additional avenues, and will continue to do so. But, in addition to the feasibility and expense of fooling the sensorium, there is the role of memory. That's the point I want to make.

A fully endowed recreation, be it of fact or fiction, is an intricate tapestry woven from diverse strands, with many of its threads capable of providing access to the whole. For me, having spent time in the navy, the cold pressure of metal against skin, the sound of an engine, or the motion of an unstable pier each can suffice to reestablish the richly real, multidimensional setting of a specific past moment and, thereby, bring it forward to the present. A light touch on the cheek, the contours of a body part or its surrogate, a musical phrase, the taste and mouth feel of softening ice cream can each go far beyond being simple sensory events. They likewise reawaken prior realities.

For the illusionist, the trick, then, is to tug on such accessible links and thereby pull out affective arousal. Playwrights and directors do it. Musicians and dancers, novelists and poets, lovers, masseurs/seuses and whores, strive for it. Artists, whether classical or contemporary, representational or abstract, have that aim, if you attend to their memoirs. Designers and chefs offer that they can achieve it. With focused research, all of the senses could someday be artfully coordinated to that end. I wish I had had the time and training to pursue that. At any rate, as I said, what we see, what we hear, that couplet of sensory modalities that are fully engineered and readily linked to an autobiographical past, must suffice.

I should clarify that by media I primarily mean the Internet. Certainly, its news, entertainments, and enlightenments are centrally managed. This has been a profound adjustment, and kept out of sight as much as possible. However, careful management has provided advantages that outweigh the justifiable distrust, its lack of privacy and control over content. From my perspective, it does offer much — yes, such as the prompt availability of movies such as *Casablanca* — that are pleasant enough.

These are sufficient to warrant ignoring the Internet's agenda-driven intrusiveness. In time it no doubt will evolve beyond representing reality to defining it, to decoupling it from any originating external. That's something to consider elsewhere. Here I'll just say that I'm not always charmed by its busy images or by the salubrious tones of its interface. Its linkages are rarely benign. Also, this increasingly dystopian world's events are heavy enough without being drenched in factitious detail.

Right?

I'm forced to admit, however, that mine may be a generational judgment, an impression not shared across all age groups. The Internet is a valid tool, a means. It exists to inform, yes, but also to sell, to entertain, and sometimes to misinform. While I understand this, it's not my profession. I'm not, as I've related, a media specialist. While I have some insights into how the brain and memory work, I shouldn't be expounding on that which creative people grasp instinctively. We all harbor a Madeleine. I appreciate that from Proust and will leave it at that. However, the Many, those busily engaged with the Now, survive quite well enough without giving much thought to these matters. I unfortunately do. As sophomoric as may be my elaboration, it has personal as well as professional relevance. Therefore, I've cause to be perturbed when I find that affective memories, often aided by media or the Internet, aren't always familiar, that they seem less than reliable. My most recent viewing of the film *Casablanca*, for example, raised exactly this issue.

More often, recently, I find certain memories more sui generis than déjà vu. This may be due to the unsettlement of age, or the result, again, at my age and situation, of having excessive time to dwell upon it. Either, regrettably, would suffice. The even less welcome possibility would be that my ability to recall is impaired. From conversations with other retirees, I suspect this isn't so infrequently noticed as it is imprudent to remark upon. In any event, the test, the validation of reality should not be via memory. The reverse should be the rule.

Well, I suppose I should refocus on my main point.

Movies become classics because of the stable truths they evoke. Whether intent is there or not is irrelevant, except in judging the worth of the filmmaker apart from his creation(s). *Casablanca* has always exemplified for me how a stream of emotive vignettes, if deftly portrayed in sympathetic contexts, can elevate even suspect narrative. Long before I retired, when having a dozen or so channels seemed a boon, if some nonattributable inner turmoil confounded my attempts to drift off, then a familiar story with a plot so porous that I could enter at any point without substantial loss, was the ideal soporific. I never was an easy sleeper. *Casablanca,* in particular, as unencumbered by weighty confusions as is its protagonist, Rick, was easy to engage. It was always sufficient to nudge me away from overindulgence in the ongoing minutiae of academe, politics, academe, money ... or academe. Right. It's that sort of environment. In any event, that film's familiar story line would dispel the miasma of vexatious, relentlessly churning, fanciful images of what had been, what is, and what will be.

I recall, many years ago when a graduate student, stumbling upon a network Bogart festival while lying about and profoundly lethargic — from strep or mono, I can't remember which — and bored with overly annotated sports. *The Big Sleep*, the sound-studio gunplay over, was nearing its conclusion. I had little sense of loss over the unseen preliminaries. Bacall with Bogart was enough. Then came *The Treasure of the Sierra Madre* (remember Walter Houston's happy dance?) and, finally, *Casablanca*! It was as affective as it was contrived. Concern with the underlying patriotic intent had long since faded. The group sing of "La Marseillaise," for example, to diminish the hands-on-hips Fascists, affirmed the back story. Nor were my lapses of attention detrimental. As the perception of movement is created by a rapid succession of stills, intermediates supplied by memory plus an instinct for continuity convoyed the film's notable dramatic moments forward.

The visual quality of streamed movies is much better than the old tapes and discs. I'll admit that. And you can get them on a whim, can follow any spontaneous urge. Yes, the logs of streaming downloads are tabulated, stored away, as is essentially everything done on the 'net. There are good and sufficient reasons for the data mining, of course, not the least of which is mercantile exigency. Right? But that, also, is another topic. I'm not going to rehash that here. It suffices to say that technological advancement provides a plethora of benefits — especially the trivial, I *will* add.

So, when I last had that urge to escape, when I wanted to watch something devoid of current themes and exhortations, I scheduled *Casablanca* for immediate view. For the most part it worked. However, after the closing credits, as I stared at the menu on the big screen, I was emotionally disoriented. The movie was cognitively familiar but did not *feel* the same. It wasn't confusion or a sense of error. Wrong was not the word, even though it left me with the powerful impression that a different ending would've improved it. That had never been the case before. It always had been satisfactory as it was.

It was a treat to again experience the novelty of black and white, the smooth, masculine Humphrey, and the gorgeous, compelling Ingrid. She doesn't appear nearly enough but when she does, oh my: the diffuse lighting, in general; that puffy delight of her lower lip, in specific; the hint of a tear. I used PAUSE several times to fix her on screen for a long look. Years ago I had come across a *For Whom the Bell Tolls* sound track long play, an actual twelve-inch vinyl original with her face on the album cover. That's it. Just her teary, far from Nordic-toned face — no title or annotations of any kind. I had no interest in the music and kept it pristine in a plastic sleeve for years.

There are numerous bits in *Casablanca* that were worth revisiting. Take, for example, the few earnest lines spoken by Annina, the young woman so anxious to escape from Eastern Europe. Her reply to Rick's dismissive, "Go back to Bulgaria," is, "Oh, but if you knew what it means to us to leave Europe, to get to America!" She overrides his sarcasm with the perfect blend of desperation and determination. And I relished the mellifluous Claude, the subtle ease with which the demigrandee is shocked by the obvious. I looked into Lorre's anuran eyes. I smiled at Sidney Greenstreet's snorts and tummy chuckles, at Kinskey's droll take on the archetypical Sacha, at Sakall's channeling of Old World attitude via Carl's artful shrugs.

The current video offerings aren't nearly as pleasurable for me. Inherently so, probably, because I'm neither a productive consumer nor a targeted viewer. Crappy tribute specials annoy me, they don't entertain. Retro-dressed *älters* feebly regurgitating instances of their former personae? Voices gone; moves gone. Bah. Totally tedious. The collections of barely rewarmed comical pap? Bah. Crime, hospital, and/or sitcom rereruns are okay, even with their sophomoric patter and recycled plots. But the device of putting the viewer in the midst of the plot, or even being ahead of the characters, is now so overdone as to be self-defeating. All of it manipulated, I fear.

Incidently, being so dependent upon the Internet, it's common to forget, ignore actually, that serious content is modulated as well as monitored to suit hidden agendas. The friend can do it as easily, and as justifiably, as the foe. But that, too, is another matter. When it comes to the full length features, however, I have to think they're stable. There would be no need to alter them. Who would bother and why? Most are mainly noise and special effects, overly loud, hyper-energized treatments for adolescent minds in two decade old bodies, and so transparent in their intention to manipulate the senses that, having lived a long life, the fakery is painfully apparent. I so prefer aged classics over banal, sense blasting, short attention span crap that –

Shit. Enough of that. That's old news.

What I'm trying to explain is that the other week, that last time I viewed the film, *Casablanca* struck me as different. That's my point. That's the core of my unease. It was familiar, but it didn't provide the ending I wanted, not what I felt Bogey's Rick Blaine deserved. Nevertheless, it was what it was.

Neither was it what I wanted for my late wife. That, too, was what it was. She, too, deserved better. After the pain dug into her and took over her, I couldn't watch TV at full volume if I passed a night on the couch. She needed every bit of absence she could manage. Muting was too extreme, since I had to be able to glean at least a hint of the emotive tonality of the dialogue. The words themselves were for that other aspect of the brain, the objective part. I could've used earbuds, except, besides being irritating, I might then not have heard her call out. Her death released me from caring tasks and sad reminders.

My feelings were unblemished by guilt; I had used that up long before. Alone in the house, I could work on lectures, exercise, read, compile lists, or even just stare at the video screen. I was unconstrained. I could explore Venice or Westwood, wander Rodeo Drive in Beverly Hills, or amble along Melrose. I could again speed recklessly through Mulholland's curves or drive north along the coast. No longer was there the need to pretend to be unaware. It was a relief to let everything go, to have dark memories freed from daily reinforcement and begin their inevitable fade. But the silence of the house eventually was itself too much of a presence.

And then came retirement. Overt loneliness arrived after the utility of routine waned and the apprehension of life as an end more than a means took hold. Superficial escapism being temporarily less compelling, I would fill a long night with an issue of *Nature* or *Journal of Neuroscience,* especially if it contained a paper in my (former) specific area of interest. I hated the realization of falling behind, of slipping out of touch with new developments in my field. I became accustomed to being alone despite that it isn't the best choice for an older person. I realize now, however, that once adopted it's hard to fully excise singularity, or should I say, reinforced solipsism. It's how we all start out, after all. It's only after having come to think of ourselves as distinct from all else and all others, after having come to appreciate the boundary of separation that we accept that there is validity on either side of it.

Again I'm digressing. Sorry. I should focus on my concerns, not on my opinions.

What I want to say is that I specifically chose *Casablanca* for that recent evening because I felt I needed it. I watched it from the absolute beginning, including the context setting voice-over and the frenetic street scenes that few would recall. I relived Ilsa and Rick's Paris romance. The upwelling of familiarity during the gratuitous insertion of Sam's "Knock on Wood" underscored how long it had been since I watched *Casablanca* from start to finish and how long it had been since I ... we ...

Anyway, after that exchange of gunfire in front of the hangar, Strasser turns back to the telephone. "Stop the plane," he barks into the handset. "This is Major Strasser! Stop the Lisbon plane, I said!"

MEMORY

The scratchy audible on the other end is garbled, deliberately impossible to understand, per ancient cinematic technique.

"Then shoot it down," he insists. "How many?" he asks without inflection, as if a census worker. "Can't be helped." There's the slightest pause before his imperious repetition, "Shoot it down.... Yes.... On MY authority!!!"

Only his voice reveals his fury. His back is to the camera, so it's cinematically up to us, the audience, to recall his prior stony, Teutonic visage. A clever and very effective evocation. The camera then tracks out, to capture the passive triad at the front of the hanger. Strasser and Renault are apart but each intent on the white gloom obscuring the runway beyond. Rick is a nonspecific crumpled heap off to the side. We are shown the oh-so-obvious scale model aircraft being lifted into painted clouds. The enhanced roar of engines is to confirm that it has reached the end of the airstrip and is attempting to climb. There are staccato burps of anti-aircraft guns in the distance. We see the corresponding flashes over the pairs' shoulders as they stare through the mist. Then come the whine, the crumply-crunch of a crash, and a faint red glow. It happens quickly, too quickly. Time and distance are improbably compressed in the damp, cinematographic fog. The reality that sound travels at a tiny fraction of the speed of light is ignored. It would complicate the scene's continuity. Hah!

MEMORY

With the full spectrum of total recall technology now in place and virtually obligatory on the Internet, gradual metamorphosis of the specific to disjointed, enhanced ephemeral impression is no longer the rule. The past no longer must grow dim. That stabilization has its obvious positive aspects. It's also in equal measure a negative, as any with painful memories will attest. Severing the bonds between present and past, which requires forgetting, can be a good thing. The young, the new generations — those immersed in their games, trivial amusements, and vacuous social probing, in the created truths of prepared news, in the past altered for cause — have less need to detach their memories. The coupling will one day be used against them, as so it is for us, the elderly. We grasp the difference. They may never.

Casablanca.

Right. Of course. That's what I mean to focus on.

Throughout those final frames after dispatching Rick, Strasser's face remains averted. Yet, his malevolence is palpable. Presumably staring into the fog at what he has unleashed, he's defined yet motionless, as in a photograph, and quite in contrast to the mobile Renault. The latter walks into the hangar, picks up a prominently displayed bottle of Vichy brand mineral water, then turns partially toward the camera as he uncaps it. With it gripped in his left fist, he inexplicably examines it from the backside. He makes no move to turn the bottle so he can see the label, nor can one imagine the contortion that would enable him to do so. He pours, then evidently reconsiders and drops the bottle into the trash, mutely reasserting his role as flexible opportunist. It's an unnecessary piece of business, dramatically inconsequential, some would judge, but an easily deciphered visual pun.

That's what life is, after all — a host of small moments strung out on a sparse lattice of major events. Those dramatic happenings are the armature, the framework, not the final, sculpted piece of work.

Yes ... Yes ...

Anyway, at the hangar, the camera's field of view narrows. We see Renault's arm lift another bottle, from beneath the table, with which to fill his glass. The camera moves in further, with the full screen Evian label remaining in focus as the final scene fades.

The film seemed fresh, almost new, as befits watching a classic. But the evoked emotions of loss weren't as I wanted. It would've been far more satisfying if Rick had won the duel with Strasser, if Laszlo and Ilsa had successfully flown off to continue his struggle. Rick and Renault should then have bonded, as the latter's adaptability and Hollywood's liberal, wartime dramaturgic logic would have allowed, to fight the Germans or to move on to some other adventure.

MEMORY

Apparently I've grown overtly romantic as I've aged. The world as it is has little room for either. The actual ending of the film was unpleasantly au courant, a virtual testimony to far-right precepts. But it was not what my selective sentimentality would have preferred.

It's frustrating to so confidently feel a truth yet be unable to prove it, even to oneself. I can't escape the feeling that *Casablanca* wasn't as it should be. What I experienced didn't affect me as I had anticipated. It seemed to have changed.

Or is it I?

A VET TEACHES HIS ELDERS WELL

There is no better clarity than that which issues from confusion.

A VET TEACHES HIS ELDERS WELL

A preoccupied Barnard slows his pace when he realizes where he is, at the patio of his favorite early-bird spot. He pauses. Then, through a clear spot in its decorated front window, determines that the also retired friend he had arranged to meet, Phil Winfree, already has company. Across from him is Martin Stoole, the hatchet faced, tedious shade from a faded past whom he'd hired and reluctantly assisted getting tenure back when chairing the Department of Economics. They're on opposite sides of a bare table — bare except, that is, for the heavy book open before Martin, which he's patting as if for affirmation. His hand hangs in midair as Barnard greets them.

"The Professor Cordner. Hello," Martin Stoole offers back. "Phil and I were having a chat. Care to join us?" Stoole's hand makes a gentle landing on the old-fashioned looking text. Barnard wishes this faintly sincere welcome hadn't been necessary. The plan had been to meet Phil alone for today's casual midweek dinner.

Phil looks up. "Hey," he says, pushing out a free chair with his foot, after which adjusting his lean, fit frame in his own.

Barnard scans the entry window's assemblage of orange and black, the pumpkins, cats, and paper skeletons of a quintessential late October pastiche, before easing himself down.

"Thanks. I will," he replies with only slight hesitation. "What are you guys into?" He examines the thick volume on the table, the rippled edges of its flexible cover, the double columns of small text on its open pages. "Anything in there about 'Thou shall not celebrate heathen holidays'?" he asks with a wave toward the decorations at the front of the café.

"Well, there is a great deal of wisdom," Martin informs him, on the verge of condescension. He taps the open pages with the tips of his thin, not yet arthritic fingers. "There's guidance that we can rely on. We need that. Especially now."

Barnard masks his lingering annoyance with the man's presence by evincing a total lack of regard for the ascribed authority of a collection of ancient, serially reworked tales. Substantially as dismissive, it's less personal.

"Instead of the tree, it's the good *book* of knowledge. Is that it?" he acerbically asks the former faculty underling.

"'Wisdom,' I said. Not necessarily knowledge," Martin clarifies without taking offense. He was always pliant. It enabled him to survive and eventually be granted tenure.

"Knowledge is what got us into trouble that first time," Phil laughs. "Eating that damn apple."

Barnard slowly rotates his head toward his friend.

"Enlightening, Phil," he says. "Right. I should've remembered you were an Old Testament expert as well as an engineer." His academician's cup of sarcasm runneth over.

"That computer logo, an apple with a bite out of it," Phil continues brightly, specifically addressing Barnard, "wasn't that supposed to mean getting a taste of knowledge? Shit. Look what it really gives 'em – a black hole of merchandising, monitoring, and misdirection. An advert for the drones. Lost their innocence, same as poor Adam."

"Well, it's smart branding," the former economics professor offers semi-seriously. "Skip the words; go for the feel."

Martin Stoole appears immune to this banter.

"There are different aspects of knowledge," he links back to intone. "There's danger in trying to be too smart, in being curious about what you shouldn't but neglecting what you should."

"Knowledge is knowledge," Barnard states tersely. "There aren't different kinds."

"Of course there are," Martin deliberately contradicts. "Knowledge is a gift that comes from faith in wisdom. People benefit from being shown what's necessary as well as what's true."

"And who decides which is which?" Barnard spits out. "Right? Anyway, how about we drop it," he firmly suggests. "I'm hungry. Food is about the only treat left for us old folks."

Pulling three menus from the side of the napkin dispenser, Barnard passes one to Phil and pointedly lays another on top of Martin's thick book.

"Never changes," the retired professor observes as he taps the plastic coated carte du jour. "Just as well. We won't have to gamble. What've you had that's good, Martin?" He senses the social wisdom of projecting this mote of contact while exploring the soft belly beneath his sport coat. What's done is done.

"The pasta's pretty good. They're generous with the tomato gravy," Phil inserts to advise. He glances at Barnard and sympathetically pats his own waist before again eyeing the choices. "Yeah, to hell with it. I'll stick with the ziti Bolognese."

Martin remains intent upon the menu, lifting it, in fact, almost to eye level.

"The lasagna's usually already made, so that won't take long," Barnard surmises. He makes use of the opportunity to give Phil a questioning look, which surreptitiously conveys his surprise at Martin's presence. Phil's shrug back is no answer but must suffice for the moment.

"I'm having something light, the Asian pork salad," Martin informs his table mates then the server, when he puts down his menu and finds she's standing over them. "Well dressed," he adds, unperturbed, as Barnard silently notes, by the inconsistency.

Their orders in and the menus back in place, the trio chat superficially until their food arrives, Each gradually succumbing to their own thoughts, they eat in relative silence. Before long Martin, an impatient eater, pushes his empty plate away and looks for someone to clear it.

"Do you have an opinion on how this is all going to end?" he abruptly asks Barnard. "The recession and the out of control federal debt."

It takes Barnard a moment to be fully in the present, to re-engage. He shakes his head to signify he hasn't.

"A good term paper topic, I suppose, but I'm finished with all that," he confesses. "And there's no one for me to lecture to anymore. Right? Except for Phil here, maybe."

"I'll say this, Barnard. There are too many taking and too few putting in. We can't continue doing that. We're going to be a bankrupt nation."

"Well said," Barnard replies evenly. "That's not exactly how I'd put it, but, economically speaking, you've a valid point. Only, my opinion doesn't matter. Rational social and fiscal policy is the government's job," is the extent of the commentary that he intends to offer. But then he adds, "They don't pay much attention to what we think, anyway.... Except maybe every four years."

"Then we have to be sure it's policy that's leading us in the right direction long-term," Martin persists, with serial looks to the other two. "We need better leadership, more business oriented people in government."

Barnard feels a pulse of annoyance, not at the sentiment expressed but at Stoole's presumption that it was his place to pronounce it so authoritatively. Maintaining a pleasant visage takes some effort.

"Yeah, you've got it, Martin. It's the government's job to lead," Phil inserts. "Even better's to mislead." Smiling at Barnard, he unzips his light jacket and leans back from his plate.

"Look at that," Barnard segues, looking past his friend. "Hutch is calling it a day."

Martin places folded hands on his lap. Silent, stiff, and stern faced, he peers through the cluttered front window with the others.

Across the street, the object of their attention bends down to adjust colorful blooms that poke out of two paper sacks. He hands a bag to his companion then touches the latter's arm and points, indicating the traffic signal. Hutch, or Herbert Porter when he was working regularly, has fallen upon hard times. He sells his handmade paper flowers to passing commuters to get untaxed cash, surviving "... at the margin," as his former occasional academic mentor, Barnard, would say. Circumstances have steadily eroded his savings.

A VET TEACHES HIS ELDERS WELL

Never satisfied working for others, a small pension soon to be supplemented by Social Security has enabled him to choose a path of independent mercantile insolvency. His nephew, Ty, who of necessity has lived with him since returning from several tours in the Mideast, contributes his medical stipend and helps with the small but modestly valid enterprise. Their complementary feelings of having made their contributions and having earned the right to be securely aided are necessary but insufficient to ensure that they are.

"There's a good example, the pair of them," Martin observes. "There are too many who've little to contribute but demand a lot. How can the government take care of people who won't take care of themselves? That sloppy fellow's not much better than a panhandler. And the other one, the kid ..." He emits a sharp exhalation and shakes his head. "We're being pushed into disastrous debt," he repeats officiously, "trying to provide for everyone, no matter what they – What's he looking over here for?" he interrupts himself to ask when the bulky, somewhat unkempt street merchant turns his face in their direction. "I hope they're not coming in."

Barnard waits until the mismatched pair has reached the near curb before he waves the invitation. His intent is that their company should, at a minimum, dilute Martin Stoole's presence.

The latter tightens, makes a similar motion to the waitress.

"My check," he tells her. "Just mine."

Even better, Barnard muses.

Martin holds out a ten and a five, nodding that she should keep the diminutive excess. Thick book in hand, he strides past the incoming pair without speaking. Ty, in particular, notices the snub. He glances down, with red-rimmed eyes, at the heavy volume firmly grasped by the rapidly exiting figure.

"And God Bless to you, too," Ty says.

"Not pleased," observes Phil.

"No. Not pleased at all," Barnard agrees, finally able to laugh. "You're out there early today," he then says up to Hutch. "Doing good business?"

"So so. Figured we'd better give it a try, though."

"Right. You never know. Well, anyway, join us," Barnard offers.

"Yeah, take a seat," Phil echoes. "Stoole's left it warm for you. You too, Ty. Have something. We'll treat."

The speed with which the new arrivals each retrieve a menu suggests that Barnard's invitation and Phil's good-natured second are much welcomed.

"Thanks, Phil, Professor," Hutch says to each. "Was that the fellow who teaches at SMC?" he directs to Barnard.

"Right. Stoole. Martin Stoole."

"Wow. Damn," Hutch exhales. "He's aged. Time sure does go by. Not a bad lecturer. I sat in on some of his, too, back in the day. A little dry." He looks briefly toward the street. "What a rotten name, poor bastard," he says before shifting his attention to the menu. "This'll be good. Been eating too much fast food."

"Thank you for this," puts in Ty, serially locking onto his hosts' eyes. His voice is unusually robust today. It doesn't match either Barnard's recollection of earlier encounters with the ex-Marine or the fit of the clothes that seem to have been cut for someone significantly heavier. "Thank you both, very much," Ty repeats quietly.

"You're very welcome," Barnard replies and returns his attention to Hutch, whom he came to know after the man had asked to audit a few classes at Santa Monica College. While obviously not of student age, he had thought the man's intentions laudable and approved subsequent requests as well.

Tyler Porter lets his menu relax down.

"I mean it, you guys. Thanks," he repeats. "An' I appreciate those other times, too. I really do. I might not've said it out lou', but I did. I should've tol' each of you guys."

He seems settled today, calm, lucid, even tentatively affable.

"No big deal, Ty," the surprised former professor responds, gratified by what he anticipates will be but a brief window of actual contact. "We're glad to do it."

"Yeah, thanks again for this," Hutch says after an equally appreciative grin at his nephew. "I'm forever fighting with Social Security about my disability. And with the VA, too, to get them to increase Ty's. Maybe add to his base stipend till he can hold a job. Any one of those'd be nice." His tone conveys a hint of self-directed derision.

When their waitress reappears, Barnard gestures for her to put whatever their guests choose on his and his friend's bills.

"I'll have the tuna melt," the oversized man quickly says. "Without the fries. An extra couple slices of toast instead. And butter."

"The cheese burger, please, Ma'am. Rare. An' fries," Ty tells the server. "An' a large Pepsi?" The latter is actually a probe of the extent of his hosts' generosity.

"It's Coke now," he's informed.

Ty looks down. Coke was all he drank in the desert and he would have preferred not to have that memory revived.

"Whatever you want," says Phil, uninformed of the full extent of Ty's experiences.

"Lots of ice then, please, Ma'am," Ty requests, looking up.

"Water for me," Hutch states. "I've been trying to cut down on the red meat," he subsequently offers to Barnard while tapping his chest with his thumb. "Clogged arteries. That's why I run out of steam so quick. We eat too much takeout and I can't afford the cholesterol pills anymore." He waves at the corner across the street. "Every buck helps. Got to do it.... My feet do go cold," he sighs, "and cramp up when I'm out there too long."

"Why don't you get some sort of job, Hutch?" Phil endeavors to suggest. "There are Help Wanted signs out there. I've seen them. They'd have insurance and pharmacy plans of some kind for you to go on. They'd have to."

"Ehhh, th'hell they would. They'd put me on part-time and give me zip for benefits. 'Help Wanted' signs? Yeah, for sure. But not mine. I'm old. Not old as you two, but old enough."

"Well, I do appreciate that clarification," puts in Barnard. "I always wondered what came after Senior."

"Anyway, what job could I get?" Hutch grumbles as if he hasn't heard. "Pulling orders in some ten-acre fulfillment center? Stocking counters at an outlet? Or, worse, working fast-food or bussing tables like ..." He stops, looks over his shoulder sheepishly, and lowers his voice. "I'd just as soon ..." Again, he lets the sentence hang unfinished.

"Well, what's so awful about a sales job? You do that anyway. Right? You probably don't net much from doing it out there." Barnard motions backhand toward the far street corner.

Hutch stares out before responding.

"Look. They want young people. Even Ty'll have a better chance than me once he gets, uhh, gets straightened out." He stares at Barnard for a long moment.

"Well, it's pretty stupid for you just to be hawking paper flowers," the latter remarks unkindly. "Working for someone else would be much better."

"Great advice. Only, a little late," says Phil, tapping his idle knife and obviously not pleased with the direction in which the conversation is lumbering.

When the two new orders arrive, Hutch looks out to scan the traffic then at Ty.

"How about it?" he queries his nephew. "We'll give it another try, after this. Okay?"

"Yup," Ty replies without looking up. He rotates his plate so that the French fries straddle twelve o'clock.

The conversation is spotty and light, which suits Barnard perfectly well. Hutch hunches over his plate, taking large bites of buttered toast to accompany the mouthfuls of tuna and cheese. Occasionally turning his eyes from one speaker to the other, Ty mostly looks out the window as he eats. Phil and Barnard linger over their plates while their guests catch up, which doesn't take long. Both are fast eaters.

"Traffic's pickin' up," Ty breaks his silence to remark. He lifts his glass and, after a substantial swallow, sets it carefully back upon its faint ring of condensation. He stares at the red-edged shard of no longer crisp potato languishing at the far edge of his plate and stretches his feet out under the table.

Hutch folds his second piece of toast until it cracks. Nestling the two barely connected pieces in his palm, he smooths on a half-pat of butter and starts to maneuver the spread carefully from crusty edge to ragged break with his knife. He spies the looks that Ty is receiving from Phil and Barnard. They each have come to judge that this seems to be an altered Ty, a Ty less agitated than usual.

"It's the new meds," Hutch explains. "They have him on what's used with the Alzheimer's people. Cognitive something something. A clinical trial deal. He's not getting the sugar pill, best I can tell." He looks fondly at his nephew. "He's calmer and ..." Feigning confidentiality, he lowers his voice, "he's not so much into the other stuff."

Barnard accepts this optimism with tight lips. He arranges what remains of ground meat and red-doused, pale sheets of pasta onto his fork. Even grown cold, he's found the dish too tasty not to finish. Phil spears his final pair of moist ziti and pushes them around on his plate to capture as much of the tangy sauce as they will bear.

*　　*　　*　　*　　*

Ty savors a sip of his Coke. His deep-set eyes take in his table mates. He's troubled and his gaze settles on Hutch.

"Don't talk about me as if I'm not here, Uncle Herb."

A VET TEACHES HIS ELDERS WELL

His voice is clear in his own mind now that he has chosen to address the two, on either side, who fail to realize that it is they, not Hutch, who are blind to the reality of what has happened, that it is they, not Hutch, who are guilty of grievous error.

"And don't you guys be picking on Uncle Herb. It's not his fault. You say you think he's stupid. But plenty of smart people do stupid things. I've seen that. For sure, I've seen that. At least Uncle Herb tries. He does what he has to do. Someone has to lose. If there aren't losers, how can there be winners? Uncle Herb isn't stupid. He's a result. He's necessary.

"You guys were there at the right time, a onetime freaky good time. Now you're happy to be taken care of and enjoy yourselves on other people's money, people who haven't even been born. And the pols? The ones writing the rules and forever raising the bar so they can spend more? They're happy, too. They never worry about the mess they make in D.C. or who's going to have to clean it up. It's all about getting themselves another term or a cushy corporate job.

"I'm not lucky or smart. And I'm no senator's son, like he sang in that song. Nope. My butt was worn down in the desert and I don't have sheet to show for it. Get trained, they tell me. Yup. If I'm lucky and will work cheap enough, then I can be like them shuffling around and staring at their little screens. What's there for me is a punk wage job and dumb-ass happy crap to buy with what's left after staying alive. That's no super deal.

"Yup, focus on the happy crap, like the 'net sots do. They sweat for whatever some shill says is rad, for whatever some site master or blogger frog croaks out is a different must-have even if it's just more of the same sheet wrapped up or tagged to look different. It's stupid, but it works. Shows what a bunch of dick-heads they've been molded into. Like mice in a lab maze. Ding ding. There's the bell. 'Go get it. Scamper to the end for it. It's all for you,' they're told.

"Run that wheel, like upright hamsters! 'Don't mind that we're watching and logging and planning. It's all for YOU! It's what you really want!' is what they hear over and over, so they'll keep on keeping on.

"Total dumb sheets.

"I sweated my ass off and watched my buddies get butchered just so I could scurry around after a dead end job here? Sir. No, Sir. I was swiping sand off my food and lips and crapping in cat holes for five years after I turned eighteen, all the time far away from the soft bodies, away from all the fun and all the must-haves they've been hooked on here. Yup, hooked like the skin n'bones shooters and those with the ugly meth mouths, like the school kids sucking on their electric tubes.

"The good jobs cost the corporate suits a lot less when they're somewhere else. Their lives — them across the border or offshore, wherever they've always been poor — move up a notch or two, and we get the dump of cheap sheet that breaks or wears out or is put out of style, all so we'll run the wheel at a mall or click through pages on a screen for more. Sure, it's no fun being chained to some offshore assembly table, living in barracks — they say dorms but barracks is what they are — and all day assembling or sewing or stuffing parts, being stared at by goons in shirt sleeves who speak a different lingo. Shoulder to shoulder and don't be talking; there's the klaxon, so go to your meal or your bunk. That's not us. Sir. No, Sir. But is lockstep hustling here to some Internet fake work or a big-box shill's pitch or delivery scheduler's time chart or order-picking quota any damn different? Is being listened to and studied, having every step planned, charted, and timed while you work or eat your meal or talk to your buds or use the head any damn different? Hell no. Time is what really costs, so it rules. Tick tock tick. The clock's what you can't buy off. Sir. No, Sir! It'll strike six no matter what. Then midnight, maybe.

Raise a toast to the guys who've made being a steady serf the smiley-face new way, despite that it's grim and older than dirt. A pretend chain is as good as a real one when paying the rent's on the line.

"Be working and still have to hustle food stamps to make it through the month? Nahh. Bull-sheet. Three jobs and no one home? That's bull-sheet too. What happened with the promise of more and more with less and less? We were supposed to be heading into a world of plenty. Wasn't it supposed to be easy and that we'd have all what *we* wanted, what *we* decided on? Not enough money to be made from that, I guess. The machines got the jobs, the ones that paid decent, anyway. They're cheaper, and better, at the grunt grind. And they don't bitch. What we got is the more and more. Too bad it's the more and more of what's been made to seem important by constant harping on fake needs. Consuming's become like a job, something we're all supposed to do, what we have to do. That's not hard to see. But seeing it would spoil the fun, which is why most of them out there are being nursed not to see it and sure as hell not to fuss about it.

"Cheaper and cheaper, more and more. That's it. That's the cadence. Hut, hut, a-hree, hut. Let the have-nots do the work, be the labor. And when they get too feisty, put robots on the line. They don't need to eat or sleep or enjoy time off. They don't bend any rules.

"Yup, most everybody's a grunt or a prole now. Only they don't feel that because of the steady drone to keep up the myths, because of the smoke machines creating the happy fog. We started at the opposite end of the game from those shabby, offshore grubbers, and we'll meet somewhere in between, existing on what's given and being happy for it. Only, not at the middle. Sir. No, Sir. There are too many for that. And it'll hurt worse for us than feel good for them, because going backward bites a lot deeper than not being there. Now it's all about making sure being happy means panting after what's been put out there and then getting it. Yup, the cheese at the end of the maze. Only, make sure their eyes stay closed and don't, don't ever let them think too much. Sir. No, Sir!

"Time was searching out what people wanted worked okay. But it cost too much and took too long and they didn't buy enough. So screw that. Making what was out there be what they wanted was better, even if was lies and silly hype. That was TV, the old way. Then the 'net took over and made that job easier, with the dumb-asses putting themselves out there for the taking, with them letting anyone who cares to take a peek find out what's made them smile in the past and where they'll look for smiles in the future. But screw that, too. With all the manipulation and nudging, with all the social sheet, now it isn't just to be sucking out what they want. Sir. No, Sir! It's to make them want what you want to give! Getting inside their heads is how to get into their wallets. And, damn, how they eat up having that be done! They're fine with being listened in on and being nudged this way and that for what to eat and what to buy and where to go. And for what's good and what's bad, too. They're fine with their little screens coming alive a hundred times a day to pitch something to know about or see. The googly-eyed 'net hustlers set it up so the sots search out what is meant for them to find. And they love it because all kinds of crumbs are thrown out there for them, because they're conned into thinking they're special and mustn't miss out, and getting it first, and for a damn dime less!

"Like the West Coast tech-man got up and said, make them crave what they didn't even know they wanted. Choice? Ha. Not when it's made to be whatever makes the most bucks. Yup, scour everyday lives and plan the choice, then infect them with it. Redefine what it takes to be satisfied. Change what the words mean. Make ketchup a vegetable and fries a meal. Make a mile the same as a klick and anybody can run it in under four. Make an inch be the size of a centimeter, then we'll all have foot long dongs! You get what I'm saying?

"All of them staring and poking sure don't get it. Sir. No, Sir. They don't think to try. That's part of the plan, too — making sure they don't try. So, it's keep them busy. Look at how now everybody's business is made into everybody's business. No point. Just is. Because it can be. Like jawing on the porch in your daddy's day. Except, no dink college sheet made big money off it then. Finding out that some ding-a-ling liked a download the same as everybody else, or that your team leader's mom's Sunday dinner sucked, or that some beet-faced jerk you hardly ever see is pumped that his squeeze was only late? Sheet. And where's the frigging big news in passing around two dogs at it, or a shot of what a first name nobody is eating, or staring at what some bimbo sent your friend that she saw and thinks is so frigging great or so frigging new? Another sunset? Another cat or skateboard trick? Another French fry or cheese snack shaped like a guy's privates?

"Sheet. Any damn thing is new or funny to somebody. So now every thought or moment gets to be a post or a pic, even if it's gone after twenty-four hours and not worth twenty-four seconds. What sorry-ass tool, besides them hustling money out of adverts or targeting their sales pitches or sticking and sucking like leeches on strangers' IDs, would do that? Most all of them, it seems like, because they fork over thousands of bucks every year to do it, without even knowing it. They're nudged to shape little hearts with their hands while the 'net masters shape their brains like some crafter molding clay. Each one of them thinks he's so important, or she does, but they're not. Not one at a time, when they have a name. But lump them all together and that's your economy working, Professor. I get that. They're what moves the bucks around and makes money for the suits and snots running them. But individually? They're sheet. Just numbers on a page and if erased replaced by another number. Yup. That's their story and they don't know it, don't ever think about it.

"Nahh. The proles don't fuss that they're being conned, that maybe there's a purpose behind it that they're better off not knowing. They think they have loads of friends but they don't, just clever, baby-faced rich pricks selling supposed-to-be private lives to the manipulators for pennies. Yup, it's like when the boss buys a fancy dinner and a couple of drinks for some sexy new intern, who's hoping to make it, so she will and won't fuss about it. The plan is that she's not supposed to care. That's exactly the plan for the whole sorry pack of 'net-staring sots, that they shouldn't care. They follow on line because it's the line they think is created especially for them and they let themselves be made glad for it.

"What's sad is that most aren't dumb. Sir. No, Sir! They're smart but still make themselves red-faced from site-diving and playing glitzy games with their buds, sometimes with buds they don't even know! They tra-la-la along never thinking that they could be tokens in someone else's game, and sure never realizing that they truly are. They never worry that what they think has value or is safe, has value or safety because someone else programs it that way. They're nudged not to worry. The trick is to seal off the worries by giving reasons, a plan, and make it that they won't or can't question. There's where the Godies slither in, like the snake in the Bible. Yup, they help make it run fine, like in olden times. Preaching What's Going To Be and hiding from What Is. Talking sideways about the Plan. Not life itself, but the Plan, the Plan that's really their Plan not His. They buddy up with the hucksters and the pols, and each does the other a favor, each makes the other's game easier, so it's sometimes hard to tell them apart.

"That about covers that solemn pecker friend of yours, the one who marched out when we came in. Not hard to spot. Sir. No, Sir. We're all sinners. Isn't that their story? That nothing'll ever go right and we're doomed to one hell or another unless we do what they say? They claim there's a way out but only they have the key.

"Sheeeet. Is it always going to be about accepting some God as *the* God, a fat book as the only reference, and then listening to and believing the ones who claim they speak for Him and for what's been set down? Is that better than looking at dried bones thrown down in front of a fire or dancing up a rain storm? We're supposed to have learned what worked and what didn't and pass it on, to have learned how to test the ops and see what held up. I had buddies die training in the desert to learn what worked. The ones who claim they know without testing, and for sure without proof, want to be in control, want to make the rules and have everyone follow *them*. But is doing because they claim they know the secret any better than having to listen to a tyrant or a dictator? Mao was a God. So was Stalin and friggin' Hitler to the people who believed.

"God is great! Allah is great! Happy Pack is great! Jeans with holes is great! No damn difference. All a sell job, a con.

"I spent tour after tour after tour being told to kill over-draped prayer-freaks because they were doing what their mullahs and what was between the black and gold covers of their damn book said to do. So here we are with our own cadre of mullahs in their expensive suits or black robes, with their own gold watches or fancy bowls and scepters, with their own stiff parchment or holy books, each with their secret archives and their own rules for what's Truth and who can have It, each tellin' the great things that you have to believe but can't see, makin' belief take on a value of its own, makin' sure everyone stays in line. Sheet.

Yup, pure sheet. I heard that over there and saw how that worked. I'm back and I'm hearin' it again, goddamnit! Those leading the pack carry on about the holies and about the basic truths and the necessary truths that are so damned easy to define because nobody finds 'em on their own. They have to be described and promised by the ones up in front, the ones who supposedly know but who really don't know, except that they repeat the same line over and over and over until it seems, in their memory of a created past, that it's always been that way, all from a long, long story that they've been given and so give out as the true reality, workin' hand in hand with the hucksters. And sure don't forget about what's happened or is happening or will happen isn't because of natural laws that they don't understand, but because of their own hand-me-down laws that they keep yellin' out that they do.

"Yup, belief's enough. That's the mantra from every earnest mouth that makes a livin' from it. That's what keeps the sucks quiet and steady. No need for proof. Proof is somethin' to fear because it's never easy and sometimes it makes a joke of believin'. I sure could tell stories about that. Yup, sure could....

"I suppose believin', no matter what, works for some. It was in their eyes, over there, when the hot metal was flyin', so I shouldn' knock it. It could work for some here, too. I'll have to take a pass on that. Only it shouldn' be a method, a goddamn tool, a mask to hide takin' control, and, yup, even murder, and rape.

"Anyway, the pols with their slogans are just smoother than the hucksters and the zealots with their scripted pitches. They write the rules and are subtler than the oily manipulators who tell that if you click on the right sheet or strap on explosives with someone else's finger on the button you can be on the edge of fallin' into happy. But they're all the same. They all tout the joy that's somewhere else and only they have the map, only they can make it happen. Work your shift without bitchin' or slackin', buy to feel good, turn every sec into an entertainment, yell hurrah in the right group, act out what's bad but's become okay on somebody's say so, mangle those who don't believe like they should — that's where it's at. They love it. Yup, on both sides, they love it.

"Sheeeet, forget that. Only, don't be laughin' at wha' belief can do. I've seen it work. An' I see it workin'. The people here aren't so different from the hate-bait bastards we were sent out after to kill over there. All wrapped up tight and beyond sweat, those over there are slathered with Truth. They're promised rich food and wine and six dozen virgins so that since they don't truly die — even though they truly do — the sandy bastards look to enjoy every sec of their coming non-lives. They believe that. They absolutely know that. But what the belief gives 'em are shrapnel vests and one-way trips to hell. Gives the people runnin' 'em a lot more and better, though. But they have to become total numb-sheets before it'll work. Now everyone here is to be molded into the same numb stuff, become like zombies, captive bodies who believe, because they hear it over and over and over, that they'll get what they've been hustled to want as long as they do what they're supposed to do and think how they're supposed to think. You guys hearin' what I'm telling you? You see how it's all a revival, the same suckin' show with a new cast, a better stage, and a cleverer director?

"The proles here — glued to their crummy jobs and their hi-rez screens, buyin' what big-box companies or other copycat pricks tell 'em is going to make 'em happy — aren't any less conned than the rag-head fanatics over there glarin' out through black slits. They're at a different spot on the big wheel is all. They'll get the same bombs and knives, the same guns, germs, and gases when the time comes, when it's their turn to feel the bite of what's happened for 'em, of what's been taken away and what's left. Weren't the rag heads the ones who did art and astronomy and invented numbers when our kin were tearin' meat off bones with their teeth and sleepin' in shelters built on poles? They fell back and were run over. Why won't we? Is oil or some machine or some computer program going to save *our* ass?

"You guys talk a lot, only you don't listen to what you're sayin'. You don't do anythin' worth bein' done. Get out there and do somethin' that is. Those pasty-faced mothers starin' at their screens won't. Sir. No, Sir! You guys should do more than search around for breakfast deals and bargain dinners, sittin' like hens an' layin' more about your lives than you actually did. Start your own damn marches. Scream out what I'm tellin' you, what you should already know because you've lived through the change. Don't cluck your tongues and be happy to laugh with the late night comic wonks who are jus' playin' with ya. Be a pain in the ass to the slutty pols. Call 'em out for giving big box suits a break on their taxes while you have to shell out more, for how they spread their legs for any dick with money balls. Sir. Yes, Sir! Tell 'em they're whores. Don't mind that their goons want to beat on you for it. Think about the ones behind you, the ones who'll know only what they're told unless someone turns it around. Think about the ones in diapers or still in hanging' sacs waitin' for hugs and kisses to send 'em swimmin'.

"Afraid you'll mess up your lives? Ha ha to that. Wha' difference does it make if it's a year shorter when you could do somethin' that means somethin' for somebody? How big's the downside of being locked away or in a cast when you're most of the way out to some gray-tiled site to do nothin' or to anyway lie in a saggy bed to stare an' wait?

"Maybe you're thinkin' some new shiny face for City Hall or D.C. will do it? Ha ha to that, too. It's Alice's mirror when you vote 'em in. They become more of what's already there is all — the self-important, pain-deaf aristocracy who think that dessert's a meal. Yup, it's a big machine an' they're the levers an' the cogs that make it work. Once they're in it, they're part of it. It's the machine that needs changin', not the cogs an' levers, goddamn it! We're racing to the bottom, to like wha' went on before, when your daddies were digging trenches an' dodging bullets. The future's what's past if someone doesn't turn it around. Better believe it.

"But, nahh, it's too late for you. There's a real bad-ass thought for you old guys, isn't it? That it's too late. So, maybe it'll have to come from ones like me who've been in a real life an' can still stand without a wobble. It sure won't be all those sots smilin' at their reflections on little screens. Sir. No, Sir. Maybe for a fact it'll be the ones who know the stink of hot blood an' bloated guts, the ones who watched their buddies become stiff an' black-faced an' stuffed inta plastic bags, who heard their last breath was a scream. Not enough of that sort, though. It's too tough, is f'sure what you'd say. But let me let you in on a secret: There's never enough, never enough who've slogged through a real life. Sir. No, Sir! Never was enough, until there was. Yup. The money-suckers know that an' they make sure to bury it. They come up with all kinds of good ways to keep it under wraps an' everyone sappy-happy.

"Yup. Yup.... Go ahead. Finish your goddamned pasta. You've got other things to worry over, like whether you're goin' to live out this year or th' next. You're goin' to die, or worse, so do somethin' while you're still vertical. Even if it's not enough, what's to lose? Maybe it'll kick-start somethin'. It's angry outliers tha' rattle the system, not sheet-faced, quieted down proles.

"I should sitfu, stuff th' whinin' I guess. It's all done an' wrapped up. Now it's be a manipulated 'net-sot, a sated serf who makes do with pretend, like fake cheese an' copycat clothes. Yup, it's relax an' enjoy it, like the gangs use'ta laugh at th' girls. Only, don' ya be dumpin' on Uncle Herb, bustin' 'im up because he turned out wrong. He did wha' he had ta. Wrong's gone. If choice's gone, then so's wrong. There'll be hell ta pay when they figure tha' out.

"Nahhhh. I shouldn' be' layin' this on ya. Ya didn' do it. But ya let it be done, goddamnit. Ya thought ya knew. Maybe ya still think ya know. Do ya??? Ya think ya can tell which of wha' slips in through your eyeballs is real an' which's someone else's creation for their own selves? Bulllll-sheet! If it's a con, then wha? Now wha? D'ya hear me? Are ya payin' attention to wha' I'm sayin'? D'ya hear wha' I'm tellin' ya, old guys? D'ya? Can ya?"

*   *   *   *   *

"Can I say one more thing?"

"Christ, no! You've said enough!" Phil instructs Barnard promptly but, as he anticipates, without effect.

"Just get out there, Hutch, and search around. Drop into places that have signs out. You'll find something," Barnard pronounces firmly. "The trick is to try, to keep at it. Something will turn up that you can do. It'll be better than waving around paper flowers on a street corner."

Hutch's butter smeared knife stops in mid-swipe. It's the tiny sign that he does not appreciate Barnard's well meant but simplistic advice.

Almost in unison, Phil and Barnard lift the last bits from their plates. They glance aside at Ty, who picks up the residual bit of French fry and chews it slowly.

"What's he going on about?" Phil asks.

Hutch assays his nephew. The worn vet's shoulders, earlier pulled back and straight, have slumped.

"Another flashback, I suppose." His expression blends curiosity, anticipation, and familial responsibility into a show of fond acquiescence. "I don't understand much of it when he mumbles on that way."

Hutch puts down his folded, buttered bread without taking a single bite.

"Time to get us back to the store," he says wryly as he stands. "Thanks. This was great. I, we, appreciate it. Come on, Ty. Traffic's picking up. We should be able to sell a few. Let's get to work. Ty?... Tyler, let's go."

Phil and Barnard watch them exit. Both are silent, introspective for a long moment. Turning his eyes back to his friend, Phil nods several times. Barnard lifts his chin and puckers his lips in the manner of a wise professor.

SUNDAE NITE AT SUNRISE

It's never too late until it is.

SUNDAE NITE AT SUNRISE

Eddy sets a steady pace as he climbs the stairs to the activity room. The two flights aren't merely doable, they're proof. He decided not to change after Harriet's service, remaining instead in the dark gray, single-breasted suit — 100% wool, faintly striped — that he had put aside when stuffing boxes destined for Goodwill. One of his finer suits, vanity had compelled its retention, vanity and a wish to remain distinct, to perpetuate his preferred self. Its classic English tailoring hid the flaws of his aging frame. He had always shunned slim-cut, lightweight suits, those seductively offering the sheen of Italian fabrics. Business uniforms, he had called them, preferring his office attire to be more conservative.

"Quite a crowd," the surprised Eddy murmured as he approached the interment site. Surprised by a twinge of envy, he moved closer to those seated at the edge of the green and white awning looming over a cradled coffin. He could have joined them, since she is, she was his aunt, but he chose not to. The midday warmth coaxed him to instead drift to an island of shade off to the side.

"Oscar, her husband, died quite some time ago, isn't that right?" he asked of an unnameable face.

"Yes," the face replied, "fifteen years." It solidified the estimate with a gentle oscillation of assent but provided nothing more.

His aunt had spent her final years with her son and daughter-in-law, a situation for which Eddy has no empathy and absolutely no inclination to emulate. But it was not fifteen years since she was widowed. Oscar left Harriet alone for the last time at least seventeen years ago, also in late June. Eddy worked that out later, during the return drive to his apartment at Sunrise Manor for Seniors, while submerged in the confines of its van and lulled by the noise from the road. He could not, however, put aside that so many showed up for her. Never close, he knew little about her social life except that she had been very active in the Rotary, even into her eighties. "Were they all from that?" he inquired of the adjacent empty seat without embarrassment.

He sighed and looked out the moving van's window, allowing the images of his children and his late wife to mingle with the passing scene. No large crowd will show up for him, he was cued to muse. A few acquaintances might attend to offer condolences. Someone of his blood will find a priest to say a few words about whom he knows little of, about whom little need be known. And then the memories of him would gradually fade.

After his return he poked at the light dinner he threw together and set out on the two seat table off the kitchen in his compact fourth floor apartment. He wasn't really hungry but knew he needed something in his stomach before the sweets of Sundae Nite downstairs. This event is held in the multi-use activity room on the floor below, so his plan was to take the stairs and thereby get a bit of much needed exercise. But first he wanted to check his mail box in the first floor package room again. This *is* Father's Day weekend, after all. A card or two could yet be in transit. The three flights down were easy. Going down always is.

Eddy could have taken the elevator up to the communal room on Three. But that would've been too slow, he decided, its walls too close and its smell too institutional. In addition, he truly needed the stairs today, the three flights of quick-step descent to dispel his lethargy and the mild exertion of the climb to Three to reassure himself.

He glances at the single, west facing, high-set window as he paces up the metal-edge concrete stairs. The textured glass and the overlain rain-streaked film of grime compromise the light from a low sun, allowing in just enough to pleasantly warm the side of his face. He senses it's time to forgo wearing suits. Except, it's Sundae Nite, his now singular opportunity for the formality of dressing up. The five years since his residential relocation is too brief a span for him to have acquiesced to the endemic unconcern that lubricates time at Sunrise Manor. Perhaps, he ungenerously considers, they should have named it Sunset Manor, but that would have been too obviously cruel, too close to the truth when coupled with "... for Seniors."

His in-breaths are measured and soft. Moistening his lips, he detects a salty tinge. He would prefer to believe this is from the coastal breeze, which he has always favored, but knows it's really a result of his many samplings of small bites and salty snacks at the reception following Harriet's service. Even though slight, that residual is a link to the sea and the memories bound to it. He has encountered many such evocative links to his past in recent months and is not sure why. Approaching the third floor landing and its glass door, he peers along the waiting hallway. Extending into the distance and lined with opposing pairs of numbered doors, the empty corridor comes to him as a parable of his productive life: There had been many doors from which to choose, what lay behind each subject to discovery, rarely prediction.

After his pause, he starts toward the bright opening at the far end. It's a third Saturday evening, another Sundae Nite at Sunrise Manor, that monthly event when those who are inclined to be sociable gather for sketchy conversations of recent events, personal as well as newsworthy, which, despite their superficiality, constitute a form of renewal. There are tables laden with cake, ice cream, and cookies, and a selection of soft drinks, coffees, and teas to make the gathering more inviting. Sometimes local folks — rarely paid — show up for a forty-five minute hour of jokes, tricks, or songs. Not today,

SUNDAE NITE AT SUNRISE

Eddy is content to discern. Such have never been much of a treat for him and may never be. He has passed through resignation but hasn't quite reached acceptance. He would prefer to be elsewhere, to be at his old house even if alone, to be those few familiar blocks from the beach where he enjoyed the unplanned pleasures of SoCal fall sun, winter rain, spring fog, and summer crowds. However, his house, his car, his deciding of the what, the when, the where, and the with whom of his activities, entertainments, and meals, all of that which highlighted their lives together then that brief, poignant interlude of regained but unwished for singularity, are behind him. His compact apartment is a place to live, a place to be. A place to wait, perhaps.

Eddy can easily rationalize that it's for the best. It helps that he's relatively lucky with his health. With good posture ("Stan' straight der, sailor!" he has frequently revived), good genes, and with the energy and balance to have moved rapidly down the three flights of stairs, Eddy's appearance hasn't changed much since the sale of the house and the move. That is his selectively validated opinion, at least. He can recall smiling in response to a cheerful "I don't believe that," or a "My, really?" at the pharmacy, at an Early Bird seating at some café, or when deconstructing history with a resident or newly hired staff. Not reliable accolades, he grants, but relevant, noteworthy.

SUNDAE NITE AT SUNRISE

He's noticed, however, that such pleasantly polite assessments have come less reliably the past year or so, which is no surprise were he to be honest about it. Simply ignoring his calendar age has become harder. Negating those kind remarks, and certainly his preference, there are the reflections in storefront windows and the undeniable, undistorted morning visage in the full length mirror on his bathroom door. Appearance is indicative even if not final. It cannot be ignored even if, especially if rationalized. Furthermore, Eddy has more concrete evidence of the burden of aging. He feels its heaviness now. The easy walks seem longer now. He seldom overtakes, is more often overtaken, now. Using the stairs this evening is indeed a test. And being driven home after the funeral, this very afternoon, provided another, that more mental than physical. He found himself repeatedly working out that this Saturday evening, not the Saturday next, was his Sundae Nite. He wasn't confused. It was that he needed reassurance. Eddy appreciates that uncertainty is more biting than is forgetting, for of the former a sentient person always is aware.

His apartment seemed dull after his haphazard meal. Because of this he vacillated and felt a need to investigate the gray mood that reflected recent realities. Standing by the kitchen entry, he looked over the comfortable but foreign furniture of his living room. Any piece from their former home would have evoked memories. All were better left behind. Even the minor acquisitions, the evidence of having lived a life, of having it mean something, which he found he could not bring himself to part with, he sometimes finds too memory laden. Five quiet, often silent years are insufficient to have excised their power. In truth, he would not wish them to be thus diminished.

Sitting near the open window, he enjoyed the touch of the breeze and attempted to open himself to the sounds of the neighborhood. He raised his eyes to follow the few gulls that chose to venture so many blocks inland, thinking: Why? Is there really something specific they're seeking? Or are they merely following habit, instantiating some instinct he can relate to but never fathom?

Eddy is a solid, practical, unmelodramatic man. His early exposure to naval order and regimen, the top down plan of it, had suited him. He prefers nonfiction, reads the New Yorker, and the long articles in the Sunday Times magazine. He has composed pithy commentaries on world events to send to the local newspaper. However, he has become increasingly sensitive to the shadows from an unalterable past and less engaged with current history's unfolding. Blurred embellishments of pleasant remembrances can be the preambles to quiet sleep but not so the failures, the missteps. When these emerge they make his face hot and sleep difficult, fragmented at best. Eddy's acceptable present must often yield to those less welcome intrusions. Their persistence is fatiguing, not unlike the gradually intensifying stress of a submariner's prolonged patrol, images of which also seem to have been revived. While the details of his subsequent commercial career were quite different, the reinforced hierarchy, restrictions, and protocol inherent to mid-level management were much the same. The parallel residua of these two phases of his life are thus mutually reinforcing and cast similar shadows.

When finally he retired he promptly came to enjoy the loss of structure and obligation. Many do not. He, however, relished these and elaborated upon the explicit freedom they provided. Miriam understood. She amiably tolerated his desire to explore, to prowl the parks along and overlooking Santa Monica Beach, the Third Street Promenade, or, when weather dictated, the malls. Sadly, she hadn't been allowed to share that with him for long. Later, alone, striding amongst the poly-clad taking their exercise, eyeing people arrayed on compact porches, investigating alleys with their discards and stores with their cheap goods made by underpaid children abroad, and strolling firm beach paths became passable alternatives. Eddy would so have preferred to stay in the home they had created together. He had projected that he could overpower its sudden, inescapable emptiness. But there had been the firm shakes of well prepared heads.

"No. We don't think you should, Dad. Not a good option," Barry had said.

His son had already determined that the house was too much for an "elderly person" to manage alone. He wanted to be sure his father wouldn't be lacking for assistance if needed, for the oversight that he, living half a continent away, couldn't provide.

"Make the best of it, Ed," his daughter-in-law had inserted, incidental to the focus of their discussion. "Get a nice cozy apartment in the neighborhood you're familiar with. You'll be happier that way, find it more pleasant."

Eddy knew what that meant. But, grandchildren or not, he, also, had no wish to be a serviceable but ungainly appendage to their busy lives. The inevitable had devolved to the incontrovertible. He has never seriously revisited the essence of that decision.

Pushing open the heavy glass door, he heads down the hallway to this Sundae Nite. His suit, his shoulders going back, his brisk march — all are to regain what he feels he may be losing. Eddy marches smartly to demonstrate that he isn't declining, that he won't allow it, not he, who looks good enough at 74 to be taken for a young 62.

Near the end of the long stretch of closed doors there is number 311, Julie Chen's office. She is the Resident Coordinator, the singular person charged with taking care of residential details that semi-independent seniors might find vexing. She helps with appointments and paperwork, for example, with issues related to the A/C, the Internet, or cable service. Wisely, she stays out of family matters. There are visiting counselors for that.

Across the hall, before the lit Activity Room at the end, is the Physical Therapy area, which is surprisingly well outfitted. There are treadmills and stationary bikes, steppers and resistive machines, single-hand weights and balance boards. Much of it superfluous for the vast majority of the residents, the array facilitated accreditation, as Ms. Chen had taken pains to inform him, and the opportunities for subsidies that came with that. Exercise helps Eddy stay fit so he endeavors to enjoy it. At five feet nine (shrinking), he judges his 168 pounds (a fortuitous weigh-in) present a pleasing profile (for an older gentleman at least). Contrary to the evidence of several waistbands, he's certain he's in better shape than the vast majority of the other residents, even those peers significantly younger. He likes to think that using the machines and modest free weights a few times a week are sufficient to keep him fit and reasonably trim.

Eddy glances in on the silent, empty exercise area. That's how he prefers to find it. Sadly, this has become less likely of late. Everyone, of course, is encouraged to do something physical, perhaps use a treadmill, at least twice a week. "But go slowly," they're now admonished, "unless Doug is nearby." There's the rub, as Hamlet was made to say. Eddy detests that individual, that ersatz aide. Because of him it's becomes too easy to skip working up a good sweat, too easy to justify avoiding formal exercise entirely. He can't understand how that crass, offensive, overweight boor suddenly was labeled an "assistant." Merely because Doug keeps watch, helps steady, or suggests the obvious, they've given him a cubicle, an almost-office, in a corner. So what if he was once a semi-pro athlete. They should have found someone from outside, a professional or, at least, someone in decent shape, Eddy again finds himself posing.

A year younger and now taller than Doug, Eddy wishes he could expunge the pushing and the bumping and the hectoring from the more rapidly maturing Douglas (as it had to be then) in high school. Eddy even had given him his Best Camper medal one September — a double fool: (a) for wearing it that first week of school and (b) for thinking it would appease.

"Here, I don't want it," the then light-bodied Eddy had lied in reply to the covetous stare. A rough block into his open locker was his reward. The coat hook bruised his temple. It could have been worse, much worse.

Absentmindedly smoothing the hair on the side of his head, Eddy is suddenly, forcefully thrust into the exact moment of the maneuver, plucked from some gritty war or gangster film, that the acne-plagued bully had used to stun an unfinished ice cream cone from his hand on a distant warm afternoon in front of the haberdasher next door to the Jokes & Magic store. It was gratuitous, viciously opportunistic, and, more significantly, energized by the fact of their disparate sizes and demeanor, in addition to inherent malevolence.

Eddy had enjoyed watching the by then already fading craft of steaming, shaping, filing or brushing, then inspecting and carefully putting aside the renewed dull domes that he expected to acquire, eventually, but never did. Unwisely, he used the diminutive form of address outside of class that morning. "Doug ..." he had started. The then Douglas didn't care for that. Only those he assigned, his friends, were given leave to do so. In front of the hat blocker's window after class that afternoon, his back to the hats and to the silly gifts and gadgets of illusion adjacent, he had pushed hard on Eddy's shoulder.

"Wanna a rabbit?" the then Douglas had asked, certain of Eddy's ignorance. Eddy took the palm-up strike with no response except that of staring down at his cone on the sidewalk. Often something reworked on sleepless nights, the feel of that moment is resurrected in the dim light of the hallway. It has become Eddy's mnemonic, his surrogate for the multiple insults and impositions that punctuated his history. Eddy never would have taken the apartment had he known the pustule was living there. And now he must accept the man's presence when he intends to work out.

He hears his constricted exhale and straightens again, his face exceedingly warm.

"Forget the bastard, already," he speaks softly though narrowed lips, knowing he's alone. Got to keep active anyway, he inwardly vows. He cups his hand and rubs the side of his neck, thinking of the exercise equipment. "Tomorrow, for a full hour. Before dinner."

Julie Chen's office door is closed. He glances at its threshold, to see if a glow reveals she's at her desk. No, not tonight. She's been a curiosity, a focus for reflection for him ever since that revelation of the need for "A Credy Tashun" as a link to the availability of secondary funds from the state. He occasionally invokes that part of her introductory in an attempt to pinpoint her accent's locale. Deliberate, retentive, a compulsive counter who has noted each of the eleven office doors (as he did the fourteen, then twelve, landing, fourteen then twelve again steps on the way to Three), Eddy has never lost that moment of his initial visit. It's a unique memory, a tethered buoy that marks the start of a new and different leg of his journey.

"For Ah Credit Tation. Yes, yes," Chen had explained to them (Eddy plus elder son Barry and his bride) when they peered *en masse* into the cold light of the exercise room. "Ahk Redit Hatian" he sometimes believes he heard. Or perhaps it was "Ahk Ready Tation." The tonal ambiguity of her comment has remained for him to dwell upon long after its significance — real or imagined — has waned. It's an image that defies time. His replays of it are, in fact, pointless perseveration. But Eddy needs such neutral ponderables to augment his meager stock of positives and, therefore, indulges them.

Eddy, while demonstrably insular, has scant inclination to spend time watching TV, except for the news and, on occasion, the financial channels. He finds its flickering unrealities devious and fraught with hidden agendas. He chooses to read. He uses the physical therapy equipment — curls ten pounder and climbs virtual stairs — and takes long real walks. Word puzzles, to exercise his mind, have become more important to him recently. Also, in common with many of his peers, he finds food a resilient and accessible pleasure. He therefore consumes his generally solitary meals in slow, appreciative bites. He will take the van to launch expeditions for which he has neither explicit plans nor expectations other than perhaps finding a new, inexpensive café. A spicy, crisp taco, a juicy burger enveloped in paper, or a tangy gyro drippy with tzatziki sauce makes a fine lunch. Breakfast out? A thick slice of freshly cut ham adjacent to runny eggs? When too irresistibly in mind, he'll attack the ten blocks to the deli for this overindulgence. Outranking all, however, is Eddy's hankering for sweets, particularly ice cream. Spooning it out from a prepacked carton isn't celebratory, it's perfunctory. It's more functional than fun. Sundae Nite is special, an opportunity for a cold, creamy, embellished dessert reminiscent of an ice cream shop.

He shakes his head lightly to either side, working his lips against each other in anticipation.

On a good day, his apartment and the relative solitude has become almost pleasant for Eddy. The promise that the former would be comfortable and adequate, with few constraints, has largely been fulfilled. He can allocate his time (energy?) as he prefers, without negotiation. His several rooms provide a better than average view over the rooftops. He can expect breezes that are not overly redolent with other peoples' kitchens. Plus, the neighborhood has remained relatively safe. He can explore about as his mood strikes him. It was his good fortune to find the bright spirited Jeanette to share time with. He hasn't forgotten how to be sociable. If death doesn't intrude, he'll continue to enjoy her company for a private meal, for an evening of TV or sketchy revelations. Each of them will age and progress — the staff's term — up to Five or Six, to become stay-at-home clients. Not yet, though. No, not yet. And Seven? The apical Alzheimer's wing? No, Never. No Zombie Zone Zeven. He's pushed that irrevocably aside.

Eddy notes that his breathing is uncommonly rapid. Perhaps he's walking too fast or is thinking too much. Perhaps it's the stagnant air of the hallway, warmer on a weekend night with the AC turned up. In any event, he can make out the subdued murmur of many slight voices from the big room ahead. He's about to enter when he sees that troublesome shade from his past.

"Shit. God damn him," hisses Eddy.

Doug is standing inside the opening with, if memory serves, his nephew.

"Goddamnit."

Hesitating, Eddy takes a few shortened strides then tacks down the side hall to the men's lav. He's already gone at his apartment. It'll be a feeble, reluctant stream now, he expects. It is. While washing his hands, he makes a point of visualizing his not too distant ice cream treat in order to subvert further concern with Doug. Behind, the urinal continues to weep.

"Damn," he exclaims. "God DAMN it!" The face in the mirror takes on a darker hue. "Cheap, crappy, porcelain, chrome topped piece of crap!"

Feeling the dull throb and heat of his annoyance, he tightens his lips and slowly oscillates his head — right, left; right, left. Turning about, charging the urinal, Eddy jams the lever up, then down; up, down, up, wishing he could break it off so that they would be forced to fix it. Finally, the cascade into the stained bowl stops. He stands for a moment. He looks at his hands then lays palms, damp after the stiff, brown paper towel, against his hot cheeks and focuses on his heavy nasal rasps.

SUNDAE NITE AT SUNRISE

Anger was once a good thing, a useful tool. No longer. It's become a pointless relic that he's been unable to discard. However aroused, it demands satisfaction, some concrete triviality upon which to discharge itself. The fact is that he's known for some time that, of the three, only that middle urinal is prone to malfunction. Trial, reaction, and release. Every time. There is that need. If only real problems, problems not intentionally instigated, would so easily succumb.

From the threshold of the wide, double doors, Eddy looks over the crowd. It's finally easier for him to mingle at Sundae Nites. He now seldom catches a glimpse of Miriam's face in the distance, sees her pulled-up hair from the back, or lifts her scent out of a group despite that images of her, of their shared home, of the boys as children, of the sweet or bitter events of an unremarkable life are within him and reachable. But they, even the sweet, have faded, like the old photos that reside in a box in his bedroom. They also have become spare of color and detail. Why don't all memories do that? he's often posed when trying to navigate the shoals of a sleepless night. Why mainly the pleasant? His selfish regret is that her death shouldn't have preceded his.

This Sundae Nite, Eddy recognizes he'll need to make a stronger than usual effort to short-circuit his persistent reliving of segments of his past, his perseveration and impotent dictations to self. At least Doug and his nephew are gone, he's able to determine. He samples the faint mélange of odors and wills it to elicit the aura of some special event, some favorite day with Miriam perhaps, but without success. It's the room itself, its high ceiling so different from his apartment and the rest of the enclosed spaces of the residence, that he experiences. A distinctly floral scent triggers thoughts of the old Y's cavernous ballroom. The rotating mirrored ball clinging to the ceiling and its fleet reflections on the floor then come to mind, which, his experiences as a sailor now allow him to retrospectively characterize, had made it shimmer like a moonlit, lightly choppy sea. He remembers that first corsage, for which his allowance sufficed, the fragrant notion that was pinned by an unsmiling mother to the strap over Judith's shoulder. They were strong, pale shoulders, unburdened by time. The high school band had again attempted Ray Anthony's "Night Train." After the inevitable Hokey Pokey had come the slow music.

Eddy's fingers extend. He can almost feel the satin around her waist and her warm skin. He touches his chin where it had rested in the softness of her hair. Turn, turn, step, arms out then clasped in, silently circling in the dim warmth. Bending in close, closer. Turn, turn and dip. Close again and silent. So close. Pizza in the dark, with the slap and crunch of the breakers punctuating their isolation. Close. So close and so hungry to know. Doug had ruined that also. What had meant nothing to him was a bitter loss to the nearly experienced, virginal Eddy.

SUNDAE NITE AT SUNRISE

Eddy experiences an explosion of memory, the ruddy warmth of ancient history, knowing he cannot undo any of it. He forces his mind to return to the present. It's only another today, he affirms. That's all it is and all that will ever be. It's a third Saturday, with the promise of sweet snacks and ice cream with toppings. He strains to melt forward into the slight but forthcoming satisfactions.

For him to have found Jeanette, also alone but not lonely, has to be put down as ignorant accident. He had not been seeking companionship. Neither had she, for reasons of her own. But it came and they have enjoyed each other's companionship from virtually their first casual chat.

Eddy scans for her but she's not evident at the moment. The treat tables are ahead, however, and he extrapolates from that. Only ice cream tonight, he reminds himself. No cake. Cake demands coffee, which he's repeatedly been told to avoid, especially in the afternoon or evening. As if to validate that advice, an erroneously labeled carafe not too long ago had imposed hours of chest thumping, side to side considerations of forty years of mistakes and of impositions from tens of years before that. Eddy has long been denied the traditional solid eight hours. He must get up during the night, sometimes twice, to pee. Also there are loud noises through ceiling or wall, or the less common but disturbing bustles in the street outside. He doesn't need an additional, a pharmacologic reason to be sleepless, with its relentless reiterations of haphazard incidentals looming large.

His history is replete with misdeeds and errors. any of which can clamor to be realigned. He often must tolerate the throb of his pulse in one ear then the other as he turns on a cool pillow trying to draw hot flush from his face. World events can be compulsively resurrected and points of views organized for declamation when sleep is really what he wants. Even so, such externals are never as significant to Eddy as are the ancient encounters and conflicts that require redirection or the rehearsals of better ways to have spoken or acted. This evening, anticipating that his sleep already is at risk, Eddy firmly puts aside the temptation of even unaccompanied chocolate cake. It would only enhance a problem of his own making.

"No cake and no coffee. And not too much chocolate syrup," he whispers after the overlong preamble of validation.

He fingers his cheek, feels its substantial warmth as he looks over the room. There's a larger than usual contingent of the older residents and their visitors at this Sundae Nite. Gazing about, the voices and recorded music barely registering, Eddy floats mildly apart. He extracts sequent samples of their conversations as he meanders, the visitors invariably speaking too loudly:

"... and how are *you*? Doing all right? Are you eating good? Has ..."

"... was last week. Didn't I tell you? I'm sure I did! I ..."

"Give Nana a kiss, Carrie.... Carrie! Give Nana ..."

It's not an unfamiliar scene for Eddy. Those arriving offer waves and smiles once their less mobile target is spotted. Old eyes follow them in and crinkle in anticipation, the reflected smiles of recognition forming when the visitors converge upon them. Some remain blank-faced and their visits will soon take a different course. Riding on an opposing current are the smiles and waves that unfailingly punctuate retreat. Old eyes, some having become moist, follow them out. For those departing there will be those few silent moments in the elevator. Then they'll push open the double doors and hurry down the short flight of stairs to their cars, anxious to get on with their evening. Next time they'll stay longer, they'll promise. That's the plan, its improbability a familiar burden for the visitors, its possibility sustaining those visited. In sum, it's a running sea of lone souls, couples, and families who take their respective places in a multi-generational mix of renewal, simple contact, deep fondness, and petty guilt.

Many, in fact most of the residents are not prominent in outside memory. So they visit among themselves, simultaneously looking on discreetly at groups of bonded others and channeling spectators at a pageant. A few from Seven have been escorted down tonight, Eddy determines, to be innerved by the crowd and the treats. Their familial visits would never be so public. These take place upstairs, in their rooms, where lack of recognition is less painful for those who've come, where it's possible to put aside, with heartache but without embarrassment, the implicit loss of a loved one still extant.

As he merges with other attendees on this Sundae Nite, Eddy appreciates the Russian doll of difficulties. He doesn't want to be warehoused, with stamina worn away and faculties corroding. He would rather "Just Go and Be Done." If he's lucky, it'll be his choice to make. It's too soon to know. With the seventh floor Alzheimer's wing, Zombie Zone Zeven as he uncharitably refers to it, having come to mind, he finds himself pondering how long a person would be perturbed by the diminution of self as the brain decays. Wouldn't its loss be precisely what eventually nullifies fear and obviates acceptance? He winces and tries to disallow such thoughts. Yet, cruising amongst the self-focused pairs and clusters, they penetrate to his core and chill him, much as had the cold engulfing sea when he was at the base of the surfaced submarine's sail and the low boat was broadsided by a sleeper wave, much as had the call that confirmed the doctor's diagnosis for Miriam, much as had giving the house keys to the realtor and selling the car.

Sweet treats and conversational reprise are the more anticipated aspects of Sundae Nite. For Eddy, the former are definitely primary. He focuses, therefore, on the two wooden tables that are pushed against the wall. He moves closer and spies new offerings. In addition to the usual three flavors of ice cream, the several syrup toppings, and the broken nuts, he notes there are sprinkles, pieces of chocolate cookie, and chopped gummy bits.

"Why is this night different from all other nights," Eddy chants to himself and smiles. Miriam had said that before, long before, in a very private moment. He had laughed heartily when she later explained the joke to him. He smiles as he examines the unexpected additions with scant interest. He knows what he'll have on his ice cream and assays those predetermined choices, glad for their constancy.

However, the vanilla and chocolate ice cream, the sensible overlay of dark syrup, and the chopped peanuts that he's come for, which he can already taste, will have to wait. There's Leandra and an empty seat. He'll visit with her before locating and, of course, sitting with his true new friend, Jeanette.

Show time!

Leandra. Always smiling, always alone. Her smile grows when Eddy greets her and sits. Glad, as usual, for his providing social contact — to his knowledge he's unique in electing to do so — she sets her nearly empty and, he notes, smaller dish of ice cream on her lap before starting to chatter on about her Calvin as if only breaching a pause. Early upon his arrival at the Manor he had spotted her sitting so silent and so alone. Quite without premeditation he chose to sit with her. Subsequent disguised chastisements only made him more determined to make visiting with Leandra a regular event. Miriam had confessed to him how it feels to suffer such compartmentalization, such rejection. During their first chat, a vivid memory, a moment in her life that she volunteered to share, had resonated with Eddy. It subsequently took on a life of its own. Their connection, as tenuous as it is, is hard to explain given their difference in race and what that means even now, in an purportedly enlightened age. That vague link and the associated tale of her husband, Calvin, were regularly enjoyed by each, if only briefly.

This evening he carries out his part with a set smile and autopilot nods. He can enjoy the interlude without concern, since he no longer wears a watch. The finale, he knows, will be Calvin's wonderful July Fourth on the beach, when he did forty-nine chin-ups to impress the muscular hunks who'd been holding court, smiling broadly all the while and later getting a great deal of mileage from expansive elaborations on the event at their dinner of barbecued St. Louis style ribs and sweet corn at home, showing no sign of the clogged left anterior descending artery that would kill him the following Sunday after a heavy, southern breakfast. But before that revelation, in the midst of Leandra's smiling recollection of her red-faced Calvin's almost even fifty, it came to always tickle her if Eddy would interrupt to ask, "And was he sore afterward? Did his arms hurt?"

On cue, he asks.

"Hoirt? Ha. He cou'd harly steer th' cahr. Kept it'n second alllll th' way 'cross tohwn! Almos' didn' make th' lef" toirn up th' hill to th' house. Neahrly stahlled it, the silly motuh, befo' herky-jerkyin' it inta foirst wit' his fist. Ha. He bahrely enuf lef" in him ta make th' toirn! Yhess, bahrely'nuf."

Her smile broadens as she finishes the last of her sundae. Her big laugh and resilient Mississippi lilt are singular at Northern Star and fated to remain so, it would seem with the recent change in management. Never having spent time in the south, other than short shore leaves at Pensacola, Eddy extracts unique music from her southern lilt. And then there are her splendid eyes, the way they go far left and right, sign the well-traveled course of her thoughts. Eddy smiles and nods, matching her eventual silence thought for thought. The virtually scripted, frequently performed finale has not been forgotten. Yet.

"Can I get you more ice cream?" Eddy asks after the pause.

He takes a deep breath, looking past Leandra to nothing on the wall. Yes, she might so desire. But no, she should not, dare not, cannot. A single dish of Old Fashion Vanilla Bean Ice Cream is plenty of sugar for her. He knows this but his habit is to offer. And nuts? God, no. Never nuts.

With this, Eddy imagines the cold crunch of his own treat. His query is the proper, considerate exit line.

After a moment's pause, he stands, grins down, then walks toward the waiting treat tables, past a young guest who, probably having spent a bored moment or two with Grandmother/father or Aunt/Uncle Whomever or some such, is examining his nearly emptied bowl. Eddy tilts his head, receiving a self-conscious head bob in return, before ruefully confirming that the customary bowls for ice cream have indeed been replaced. The new bowls, of pale green plastic, will definitely hold less than their precursors, which were only adequate. More troublesome, since he can always have a second helping, is that he can't immediately locate the spoons. He wonders if they, also, have been downsized. The three flavors of ice cream before him, Eddy feels again the snug warmth of the drug store on Montana Street, the pleasure of a cool fall evening when he was ten and had sufficient coins in his pocket. He's going to help himself to chocolate AND vanilla, regardless.

"Spoons?"

He repeats his interrogatory as he looks about. Ahead, he notices that Jeanette has served herself. She appears to be looking for a place to sit and Eddy anticipates that he will join her for the rest of the evening. This will complete his day. However, at the moment Doug is beside her, no doubt attempting to chat. Eddy wants to sit after he constructs his sundae but not with or even near Doug. Neither does he want to enjoy his treat alone, since on a Sundae Nite that would make him seem odd. He scans the room once more. Perhaps, he thinks, he can visit with Manny Konrad over there, a casual acquaintance in high school who is now on the way to Five or Six. Manny accepts help, is adapting to the thought of that paradoxically upward move. Giving him a bit of company, providing him a few moments of casual conversation might be another good deed, his second of this evening. Plus, it would provide a compensatory benefit since playing the audience to slow decline is preemptive, perhaps even protective. The reality of inexorable diminishment, seeing it in others, makes sudden destruction seem preferable. Fear of the former is thereby eased by the facilitated knowledge that it doesn't have to be endured. Eddy shrugs, providing that sign that he's concluded some internal debate.

Fixed in place, he notes that Jeanette is still talking to Doug. In fact, his slouching nephew has joined them. The latter — so similar to his uncle — seems poised to return for yet more. Why can't the two of them get bored and leave, go away? Eddy complains inwardly. Eddy expands the thought, recasts it as an ungenerous wish for the singular scourge to be gone for good, for once and for all, by whatever method the Good Lord sees fit to apply, but painfully, if he would be so kind. He smiles, shakes his head, and turns to create his sundae. If need be, he can tolerate sitting alone for a bit.

Leaning forward, he selects a newly inadequate bowl then spoons into it as many dollops of creamy white and sticky brown as it will comfortably hold. Having added the syrup and the chopped nuts, he resumes his search for the spoons, a spoon. He sighs heavily through his nose. Knowing they must be nearby, his tongue explores his lips.

"They ... are ... over ..." he mumbles. "Ahh. There."

He spots the clear plastic utensils at the far end, nestled together in a basket that's lined with thin paper napkins.

"Pfffhhhh," Eddy releases through tight lips.

Looking fitter than he should, Doug has inexplicably come to occupy the junction of the two long tables, resting on his thigh with ankles crossed. Providentially, his proximity means that Jeanette will be alone. He wonders if he should greet the unpleasant man, offer a curt "Hello," perhaps. It *is* a social, after all. He dismisses this idea and ignores the perched figure. Eddy sets down his constructed treat and retrieves a pair of napkins from an adjacent stack before starting the necessitated short trek for his spoon. Task completed, he turns about, the two napkins now clutched tightly in his other hand. Eddy always uses two of the thin paper wipes. One will be for his lap, the other for his lips and chin.

"Why not at the same end?" he mutters, cheeks warm as if bathed in the tropical sun of his early tours, his chest feeling the press of being submerged during Basic's drown-proofing drills. "Silly. Bowls there; ice cream there; napkins there. Spoons here. Stupid."

Eddy rightly senses that these thoughts are destined to become another nocturnal monologue, another complaint to compose on a sleepless night, perhaps tonight. Sucking his tongue in annoyance of many dimensions, he walks past the offending shadow of his past, transferring the spoon to join the napkins in his left hand so his right will be free to retrieve his sundae.

"What th' hell?" he hears himself exclaim.

It's louder than he intends. There's no treat, no faintly green, inadequate plastic bowl with softening chocolate and vanilla ice cream, dark brown syrup, and, of course, nut pieces. Could someone have cleared so quickly? Right hand extended and stiff in frustrated anticipation, spoon and napkins now clutched in the other, Eddy is immobile.

"What the Hell!" he repeats, too loudly. He knows his bowl was there, at the edge of the table waiting for him. Potential explanations unfurl as sequential rising signal flags:

The bowl fell off — "No. No spill."

The bowl was taken away — "No. No staff near."

There was no bowl — "Oh, God don't let it be that. I remember. I remember."

Eddy feels pressure building in his ears and a prickly warmth envelop his frame. The pressure extends to his chest.

Sharply and inconsonantly the adjacent figure slaps a green plastic bowl down, hard.

Thwock!

The sound of contact with the thinly covered wood top of the table is hollow and loud. Eddy can see its result, that the impact has disturbed white and brown milky residue within, nut bits only imperfectly glued to its wall by syrup.

It's his bowl!

Eddy feels searing heat fully invade his face. His mouth opens slightly — a silent fish gasp. He's momentarily confused and seeks to understand the moment.

"That was my sundae! You saw me put it there. Why did you take it?" he charges.

The lounging figure looks down at the empty dessert bowl then off to the side. Its face finally turns full toward Eddy's, its lips forming the hint of a smile. In a flash Eddy does understand. He grasps the meaning of the smirk and knows that it's not Doug, it was never Doug. It's Douglas, and it's time.

"That was a rotten thing to do, for chrissake," Eddy says. Every square inch of him seems on fire. A heavy weight sits upon his chest. He realizes his voice is loud, demanding, but he has the confidence born of his familiarity of place, of his many Sundae Nites of the past and those yet to come. He anticipates some facile excuse: "I thought they had set it out," or "I didn't see you make it," or "I thought you left it," or, and this he grants to be most improbable, "Sorry."

But none of these would make a difference.

"How does it feel to be a fading old relic?" he hears the Douglas say.

The voice is smooth. The words are distinct, blithely rhetorical, and piercing. The figure's eyes are wide and inches below Eddy's. If there's true recognition in them, Eddy doesn't see it. The busy room has become quiet, and distant and blurred. It's an active, almost crowded Sundae Nite. Yet, for Eddy, there's only Douglas.

In a quick movement drawn from Basic Training, imaginary battles, and replayed fictions, the heel of Eddy's free hand crashes against the nose above the smirk. Rehearsed in silence many times since first taught, felt in joint and muscle in nocturnal remembrances of slights ignored, of insults passively borne, this time Eddy hears it.

Crack!

"Hit the damn dummy on th' mark, sailor. Snap tha' arm ow'. Th' point's not ta knock'm ow'. It's ta make'm lose focus," the dour trainer had droned. "Ya ain't goin' ta knock ow' a big fella. Not in yar skinny ass life. Yar goin' ta try ta make'm lose focus, make'm close their eyes fer a sec. Den ya got time."

Eddy steps closer. In a single swift motion, he loops his instep behind the lazily crossed ankles and jerks them forward so that the Douglas slides down, the back of his head hitting the edge of the table, both hands en route to his face. The slumping figure is taking short, pained breaths. Blood will be coming. But not yet.

Eddy looks about. No one is attending to him. They're looking to where he was, to the tables offering beverages and sweet treats, and to the figure on the floor before them. There's no rush forward. The residents don't rush, they gather. Rushing is for staff.

The tingling has passed. The room grows hushed and dim. Eddy's ears are filled with the roar of the sea. Moving away effortlessly, as if carried by an ebbing tide, he doesn't feel its chill.

"No more Sundae Nites," he believes is in the rush of noise. He hears it as coming in his own voice. He also hears another's. "'Ah Credit Nation.' Yes. That's how she ..." he murmurs in reply.

RESOUND, THE SILENCED PAST

The future and the past meet without convergence.

RESOUND, THE SILENCED PAST

After their short, pleasant excursion to Santa Monica Pier, the two elderly gentlemen wait for their ride home. A low western sun, unimpeded by trees or buildings, caresses their napes. After leaning forward together for a quick look to their left, they stand and step up into the advert-covered bus that has genuflected before them. It will head south, turn onto Main, then, via Ocean Park Boulevard, continue up over the Highland Avenue crest and speed across Lincoln on the way to their stop near Santa Monica Airport. From there it will be just a short walk to the residence. With nonverbal common consent they take the outfacing bench seat near the center, on the driver's side, as usual. This affords them a last glimpse of the pier, its details lost in the glare, upon which they had strolled to its fishing deck at the far end.

"You're playing with your gut as if you're hungry, Jerr," Nathan states incidentally, not intending to pursue anything of significance. "From our brisk march, is that it?"

"No. Not hungry. It's heartburn again," Jerome replies blandly. He takes hold of the shiny floor-to-ceiling pole between them as the bus accelerates across an intersection.

"That little shrimp cup wasn't enough to ruin dinner," Nathan observes. "The sauce was too spicy for you?" he then suggests.

No reply forthcoming, Nathan looks across to where sits a middle-aged lady in a print dress with short sleeves. She's obviously from south of the border, probably someone's housekeeper. From her tired face and the elongate loaf of bread peeking out, she is heading home to make dinner for herself or, more likely, herself and family. Well into his retirement, with little to occupy him, Nathan is prone to extract such detailed deductions from scant evidence. Blank-faced, but aware of the intrusion, the woman pushes the bread deeper into the substantial cloth bag pinned between her legs.

Further down the aisle an unaccompanied, comely young woman stares out, tracking the passing storefronts with impartial saccades. A sales clerk from the Third Street Promenade, he decides, or a UCLA student returning to her dorm. He notes further that the several young adult passengers near her are focused on their hand-helds. Similarly dressed, the thin white cords of their earbuds crossing over concave chests, their searching thumbs and the slight working of noncommital lips provide the only evidence that they aren't statues.

"Typical," Nathan says, nodding toward the clutch of small-screen devotees. "Their necks'll get permanently bent, like coolies or old ladies," is all he can project upon them.

"It's what they do, I suppose," the usually taciturn Jerome chooses to agree after a glance. "Generational," he adds to clarify what the "they" is meant to imply.

"Download, plug in, and be perpetually amused," Nathan observes. "In our day it was simpler: 'Turn on, tune in, and drop out.' Their rewards'll be question mark torsos and arthritic thumbs. The gray hair and shakes'll come later. Good old Timothy had the better way, I think."

"Well, that completes the picture, doesn't it?" Jerome states, not inclined to pursue the matter further. "What time is it, Nate?" he asks when he's turned his gaze elsewhere.

Nathan smiles and rotates his wrist. "Ten to six," he states, then appending, "Seventeen-fifty hours." The superfluous restatement of the configuration of the big hands on his mechanical watch is meant to honor his military manner of wearing it.

Soothed by the slow rocking of the bus and the becalmed warmth, the two seniors drift into their respective personal worlds. Behind half closed eyelids, Nathan conjures up images of the riverine Brown Water Navy of his final tours in Nam. His memories of the transformative, indeed restitutive diversions of comrades and cards, coke and cigars are overtaken by an almost physical recollection of the humid and oppressive green-tinged, semitropical gloom, of the slow throb of a cruising PBR and the acquired habit of leaning against its motion, as he does now with the bus's starts and stops.

Pulling away from the curb, the driver hits the brakes hard, which tilts the two retirees toward the front, shoulder against shoulder. Nathan's eyes snap open and he looks out through the windshield. Run aground? A floating nipa palm log? Improvised floating mine? No. Some boob made an illegal right turn in front of their bus. He rests his head against the glass to enhance the vibration, to make of it a soothing sensation rather than noise, and partially closes his eyes once again. Conspiring with the gaps between buildings, the low sun contributes brief bursts of glare that play upon his lowered lids and elicit staccato flashes of maroon and brown, flickering instants of recollection. Dreamlike, these come to him as the reddish brown of blood too old to be emotive, the sun-speckled dirty brown of water of undetermined depth, and the spotted brown of poisoned leaves ready to fall. He had changed, grown hard, yet his undistinguished thereafter has put uppermost the fact that he'd survived.

Jerome stares straight ahead, unburdened by any such autobiographical fantasies. He has rarely indulged those, neither before nor after the premature death of his wife. The pressures of peripatetic technical sales were more easily managed — and, indeed, in their own way came to be compensatory — without such diversions. Having spent so much of his life talking to many, in retirement he has come to prefer saying little. In addition, this afternoon his focus is inward. Hands on his lap, he presses his thumb upon a pulse point to gauge rate and regularity, attempting to assign insignificance to his persistent fatigue, perhaps to rationalize it away. He wonders what his face, which he sees hovering upon the window opposite, is projecting and brings it into focus. Putting aside his own health concerns and what his mien may be revealing of them, he considers Nathan's reflection, the heavy lids and set expression, whether he's tired, also. Why had he never married? Jerome wonders. Too long in the service, he once again presumes. Sharing much of the last three years as proximate friends has allowed them to compile only brief and incomplete dossiers of each other. Some questions were better left unasked. A hitch in the bus's motion lures his attention back to his own image, which comes and goes as it blends with the passing urbanity.

The bus will make the coming last stop before turning roughly east to head along Ocean Park Boulevard toward the UCLA Campus, its terminus. Both men brace their feet in anticipation as the bus slows. With a soft whoosh its front door opens. Three young men carrying beach bags leap up the stairs. The ID-fier beeps for two. The driver makes no comment. Particles of sand fall from their nondescript shorts, so that the sandals of the two behind scrape and crunch as they move in line down the aisle. Each sports the same short cut hair, military. Nathan runs a palm over the hairs of his temple. No doubt, he considers, they've spent the day reconnoitering the sand, ogling the potential delights of mostly-bare young women. And not as unrealizable fantasy, he concludes, with rueful apperception of his own senior status. He raises an eyebrow at Jerome, who grins back.

The three stand bunched close, hanging onto the overhead rail, brazenly eyeing the scattering of seated passengers, as the bus accelerates into a smooth left turn.

His feet countering the thrust, Jerome grips the adjacent chromed post and scans the trio. He glances again at his friend, whose eyes seem focused straight ahead. Nathan nods slowly, in another mute communiqué of assessment, before commanding his lids to sink once more and rolling his head against the window glass to reestablish his reverie, to become again immersed in the dank, humming quiet before mine or pregnant sampan explodes at the waterline. The bus picks up speed. He's lightly touched by an ingrained wariness commingled with constant motion, by the odor of fuel blended with the spice of human closeness. When the bus comes to another sudden halt, Nathan experiences an upwelling of the anxiety and confusion formerly linked to lethal stasis. He can keep his eyes closed no longer. He opens them to see three pairs staring down.

"Sleepin', old guy?" the tallest of the young men snidely puts to him before swiveling his head about to ask at large, "Another stop already? Wha' th' fuck?" They pivot as a group, leaning down to look out through the side window. Then they focus on the unremarkable woman with the shopping bag between her feet and skin brown from more than the sun.

"Are we goin' to fuckin' Tijuana or what?" another ventures as he explores her with impudent eyes. "This is the UCLA. Are ya on the wrong fuck-ing bus, lady?"

The woman pulls her arms in close without answering.

"Maybe she's lost," he leans over her to say. "You lost, lady?"

She chooses to be painfully unwise.

"No," she says stiffly, looking up. "I am no lost."

Nathan wishes that she hadn't spoken. He feels it in every tense muscle of his body. Another few seconds and she could have gotten off, could have left them behind, been forgotten. He feels sorry for her, anxious for her, even though he does not know her.

"No lost? You no lost?" the same youth echoes with a satisfied giggle.

"Ya think she's legal?" his short, gaunt companion is thereby cued to ask in a loud voice. "Where's your state ID, Conchita? Or your green card. In your big bag there maybe? Or no?" He kisses the air above her. "Ya work more at night maybe?"

Nathan feels an adrenergic rush that he judges is inappropriate, since the woman is, after all, a stranger. It's not his place to fear for her or to be protective. Yet, it's fitting and, more revealing, automatic.

At the next stop she pushes herself and her bag past the sandy tormentors. Stepping down, the rear door swings open for her with a hydraulic hiss. On the curb, incongruously defiant, she casts a stream of incomprehensible but unmistakable invective at the three. They laugh down at her and gesture as the door unfolds to close. The driver peers into his rear view mirror, waiting, again deciding.

Foolish, foolish, foolish, Nathan thinks. So foolish. Surely she takes this bus regularly, he infers, and must realize that the self-satisfied harriers could be encountered again. Silent escape was her best course. Sadly, the path of reason is not always the path taken, not what comes most immediately to mind, and is sometimes made impossible by circumstance. Nathan appreciates that this could equally apply to him. She should not be judged but, rather, admired.

"Wha' do these wrinkly geezers think they're starin' at?" complains one of the three. Piqued by the lack of response, he addresses them directly. "Why do they let ya hang on so long an' ride free? Ya don't do nothin', don't pay nothin'. Just suckin' the planet dry. Isn't that so, old guys? Aren't ya waitin' to die and fuckin' suckin' the planet dry?" he demands, evidently enjoying the cadence of the spontaneous trochees of his denunciation as much as its substance.

RESOUND, THE SILENCED PAST

With the accusatory trio glowering down, neither Nathan nor Jerome deigns to reply. Gaze fixated on the space in front of them, Nathan's fingers have flexed inward, toward his palm. Squeezing his thumb in hard, he savors the feel of plunging the sharp fist deep into that unprotected space above the navel in front of him. He might manage it. He had done so, in practice and in sport, and so wants to hear again, now for good cause, the pained gasp. He would not hold back. He would take delight in seeing surprise overtake that face above, watching the arrogant pose behind it melt as the body folds forward and the miscreant must force himself to breathe. However, no matter the ancient training, no matter how reasonably fit he is "for his age," Nathan is no longer strong enough, nor quick enough, nor ready enough. It has been too long. He senses Jerome tighten beside him. It's doubtful, however, that he's indulging in a similar rehearsal.

. "Ya think they're kikes?" one asks rhetorically, in a proud voice. "Yids? West L.A. an' the beach cities are loaded wit' 'em. They scurry aroun' here an' buy it all up, jus' like in Florida and Jew York. Blood suckers, like lice. Shalom, you fuckin', suckin' ticks," he exclaims with another coarse laugh, not interested in receiving a reply and certainly not in need of any.

Nathan rubs his hand along his thigh with lowered eyes. He grasps who he is, that he isn't who he was. He must accept his limitations. In partial compensation, he also grasps the nature of his accusers. He intuits their unrecognized enforced situation. Young, robust, and ill-prepared, they are of the able yet barely skilled, the unschooled yet trained who are being manipulated to serve, as hand puppets, the pleasure of others. Mobilized and regimented, their individual inconsequence has become the means for others' collective strength. Along with the many other malleable recruits, these three have been schooled to relish the role that's been prepared for them. Their futures assigned, they're propelled by desires that have been crafted for them, within them and reap the rewards that come with tribal rites, which manage and use their discontent. Mesmerized by a clever drum major, tranquilized and made secure by identifying with ephemeral peers, they march in the magic circularity by which partial satisfaction becomes total. They are of the many who'll glean fields already harvested for the few, much as did the serfs of prior generations and as do the peons of this.

An unfortunate regression, Nathan muses as he strives to avoid eye contact. Voices from the past, once finally silenced, have been released to sound again. It's immaterial whether their interrogators have suffered hurt, physically or otherwise, from a Mexican or a Jew or Muslim or gay or any other of the targets mapped out for them. Despite their projected certainty, Nathan considers as he scans the young men's shoes, none of them can be sure of who or what he is confronting. Each has only the conditioning presumptions they have been given, from which has flowered a priori validation — a potent oxymoron — and its fruit, self-fulfilling action. Cajoled into accepting a sinister inoculation, they have no inking of the grim sickness that will stem from it. Worse, they are conditioned to never appreciate it as the imposition that it truly is, the very opposite of the full freedom they have been so assiduously informed is their right, their duty. Having not experienced better, they will live out their lives convinced they are being rewarded for honoring the fictive truths that have been revealed to them. These three will never seek out nor even tolerate contrary conceptions. Willing compliance is an essential part of their training, the carefully constructed armature upon which much will be laid and sculpted. Their manner is a reflection of the instrumentalism that conditions their behavior, the rationale they have been provided, and the solutions they have heard in persistent, dull drill.

Their manner, everything about them exemplify the ease with which veins of anger, jealousy, fear, and cruelty, even if overlain with familial goodness, can be mined for dogmatic, authoritarian-centered gold. Only a self-ratified platform from which to enunciate the malignant orthodoxy is required — plus, of course, the readily assigned cadre of victims upon whom to focus their discontent.

Nathan has been propelled into his past and beyond, into an ancient past revived and so revisited. He had endured violent villainy up close as a young recruit. Then new to him, his appreciation of it was viscerally concrete. He has, therefore, a right to conceive of it as not preordained. He knows there can be better. Yet, if only it were really that simple, he further considers. Never dead, merely sleeping, hate has been awakened and given direction.

He would be gratified to learn that some ill-perceived sense of emptiness, some vague appreciation of their own dim prospects, some faint sense of decency remains within them. The strain of an instinctive awareness of its suppression could be the basis for the antipathy that has been so artfully choreographed, an antipathy molded and extracted, called forth as might be an actor's performance under the guidance of a skilled Method director. Therein would lie a glimmer of hope. Their vigor thus could some day turn against their angst's true origins instead of remaining in the service of the current manipulators' carefully crafted falsehoods. Nathan savors this optimistic paradox, this latent seed of inevitable self-destruction. He knows, however, that any resolution will come well beyond his own end.

"Naaah. Just old. All these geezers look like kikes. Smell like 'em, too," says the shortest of the pack. He bends close, his eyes just above the docile sojourners, and sniffs each coarsely, twice. "Old, dead farts. Stinky. Like old clothes."

"Stinky old farts," giggles an associate.

RESOUND, THE SILENCED PAST

The bus pulls in front of a waiting group of four. Rising with Jerome to file out, Nathan trails behind. The muscles of his face, earlier simply tense, are on fire. A hard hip slams into his side as he makes his way to the rear door. He offers no objection to the gratuitous act, coming as it does from a to be pitied youth who's destined to strive laboriously for what he's allowed to have. Forever indentured, Nathan thinks, and accepting. Who will be the true losers? he reflects between heavy heartbeats. We? She? They? All are arguably victims.

How he would delight in declaiming their profoundly empty future, their fostered ignorance, their slavish absorption of half-truths and full lies. Even if it were only to fall upon deafened ears, the declamation would gratify him, relieve him. And how he would love to give as he has been forced to take. But far, *far*, FAR superior to words, his every muscle aches to have again a sharp or powerful tool with which to rework the imposition. But these young men have no fear of retribution or castigation from their targets. They have the advantage of being untroubled by what they might or might not have provoked. Negative anticipations have been, if not excised from their repertoires, rendered impotent. Provocation is their purpose because through it presumption becomes fact, action is provided justification. Reaction, of any form, is doomed to failure because it is itself the goal. What will be worse for them than enemies is when there are none, when history does end for them. With any assignment of right or wrong moot, they will have nothing. There must be both to grasp the nature of each and to have purpose.

Nathan expels a long sigh of resignation as they walk toward the residence. There is little else for him, for either of them, to do. It's all a matter of faith and circumstance, which are idiosyncratic, and history, which is rewritten in accordance with dominance. Through the window of the departing bus, they watch the trio, their hands skimming along the upper handrail, sidling toward the young woman. The last they see is them leaning down, their faces close to hers.

"You wanted to punch him in the balls, didn't you?" Jerome interrupts their silence to observe. "I could feel it."

"In the gut. The plexus here," he says, thumbing the space beneath his sternum. "So, 'round and 'round it goes," Nathan then offers.

"What do you mean?"

Nathan doesn't reply to his friend's quite reasonable puzzlement. Further conversation on the incident would be unsatisfying, vacuous, it seems.

"Did you get which driver that was?" Nathan inquires.

"No. And I don't care," is the terse reply.

"Right. No point," Nathan agrees. "Surfers to serfs, in a single generation," he adds for his companion's enlightenment. He alone smiles; his friend seems to accept the superficial pun as ineffable truth. "Let's hope we don't run into them again."

Jerome nods silently.

"I feel gritty. Need to shower before dinner," he eventually remarks as they cross the quiet street to their residence. "Going up?"

Nathan shakes his head as they part company. He waves vaguely and heads toward the common room. It's empty. Everyone must be at the meal service. He faces the busy TV screen, watching the alternating talking heads but not hearing what they are saying. With a shrug, he turns sharply and returns to the elevator. He needs something other than information or entertainment or food to expunge the last half-hour, to preclude the sleeplessness that he senses looms before him.

Pausing, once the bright metal door has slid open, Nathan tries to gauge his true intention then watches it close. Being alone isn't what he would prefer this evening. He retraces his steps, heading for the dining room where he will have a fractional dinner. Hopefully, there will be an opportunity to immerse himself in familiarity and find out what has gone on today.